THE DARKNESS AT DECEPTION PASS

A THOMAS AUSTIN CRIME THRILLER
BOOK 9

D.D. BLACK

A Note on Setting

While many locations in this book are true to life, some details of the setting have been changed.

Only one character in these pages exists in the real world: Thomas Austin's corgi, *Run*. Her personality mirrors that of my own corgi, Pearl. Any other resemblances between characters in this book and actual people is purely coincidental. In other words, I made them all up.

Thanks for reading,

D.D. Black

I have always been fascinated by the ocean, to dip a limb
beneath its surface and know that I'm touching eternity,
that it goes on forever until it begins here again.
—Lauren DeStefano

Making the decision to have a child - it is momentous. It is
to decide forever to have your heart go walking around
outside your body.
—Elizabeth Stone

It's not the fall that kills you; it's the sudden stop at
the end.
—Douglas Adams

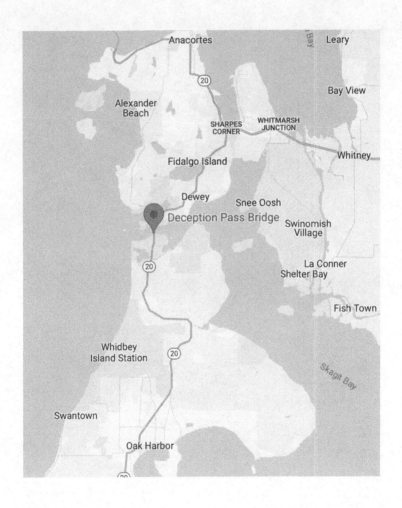

PART 1

A DECEPTIVE CURRENT

CHAPTER ONE

The Waters Beneath Deception Pass Bridge

Between Whidbey and Fidalgo Islands, Washington

Monday

WHAT A BOTTOM FEEDER!

Ben was the first guy Carla Rivera had dated since her breakup with David, and she was already regretting it. What was it about men that they couldn't for one moment admit to being the lesser scuba diver? Maybe it wasn't men in general, she decided as she swam past a bed of kelp, just the losers she attracted.

She let out a long breath, bringing herself back into the moment. Vibrant plumose anemones clung to the rocky seabed a few feet beneath her, their colors muted but striking against the dim light filtering through the water. She spotted a curious lingcod lurking in the shadows, its mottled skin blending seamlessly with the surroundings, and marveled at the intricate dance of life happening all around her.

It was a gorgeous day in and out of the sea, and perfect for a dive. The problem was, she couldn't enjoy any of it. She was still too pissed at Ben.

After arriving late, he had complained about the gear she'd brought him, despite the fact that it was top of the line—a Scubapro Hydros Pro BCD, which provided exceptional stability and comfort and an Apex XTX200 regulator for smooth, reliable breathing. Not to mention the Atomic Aquatics Split Fins and top-of-the line drysuits. She was even wearing a brand-new Aqua Lung dive computer and body cam, ensuring she had all critical dive information at her fingertips and that they could watch their dive later from the comfort of her Whidbey Island shop, *Dive or Die*.

She looked to her left and saw Ben about twelve feet from her, fiddling with his monitor. She swam a few feet in his direction to bridge the gap. As much as she didn't like the guy, she always maintained buddy-system distancing.

She smiled to herself, happy knowing he couldn't see it. She wasn't going to forgo a chance to enjoy the dive, even if she had to swim alongside this clamped-fin guppy. She reached her arms out and arched her back, moving three dimensionally in ways that weren't possible on land. Feeling the weight of the saltwater on all sides like an embrace, she allowed her tensions to melt as she watched the schools of rockfish dart in and out of the anemone formations, their scales shimmering like liquid silver.

Above her, kelp forests swayed rhythmically, their long fronds creating a mesmerizing canopy that filtered the sunlight into a beautiful, otherworldly glow. Carla felt a profound sense of tranquility envelop her. Despite its unpredictable and sometimes treacherous tidal activity, she was reminded of why she loved diving here. No matter what was going on in her life at the time, here she could tap into a feeling of transcendental peace. The only other place she felt this way was at church on Sundays.

Gliding effortlessly through the water, Carla's eyes were drawn to a cluster of giant Pacific octopuses nestled in a crevice, their movements purposeful and measured. Generally solitary creatures, it was something special to see them gathered together. The area's marine life activity likely made for an abundant food source, allowing them to live in close community. She watched in awe, taking in every precious moment, as one of them extended a tentacle to explore a nearby sea cucumber, its delicate touch a testament to the creature's intelligence and dexterity.

Despite her irritation with her partner, she turned excitedly to point out the scene to Ben.

Where was he?

She signaled him on the electronic device.

Nothing.

He wasn't showing up on the receiver, which meant his equipment had malfunctioned or he'd decided to turn it off.

She swam a few feet in the direction she'd last seen him, before she'd been distracted by the octopuses. Staying calm so as not to deplete her oxygen, she immediately implemented her training.

She performed a methodical, 360-degree scan of the area, careful to keep within viewing distance of the consortium of octopuses, then scanned again.

No Ben.

What part of the buddy-system had the man not understood?

In diving, communication was key. You always stayed

within six to ten feet of your diving buddy, and *never* surfaced without telling someone.

That's probably what he'd done, she told herself. Most likely, he'd still been upset about the gear and had left for the surface in a huff. As she searched, she tried to set aside the fears that Ben was in real trouble. Given what an arrogant jerk he'd been about the equipment, part of her wished he were.

Not really, of course. Her mother often told her, *strive to be more like Saint Rita*. That's what her mother had always done with her abusive father. But last time her father had beat Carla—instead of invoking the saint of lost causes and difficult marriages as her mother recommended—she'd run away. Having grown up exploring the Belize Barrier Reef, she couldn't remember a time she didn't long to escape her father's wrath for the ocean. So she'd escaped to Mexico, then moved to the U.S. on a tourist visa and eventually settled on Whidbey Island, where her diving expertise was valued by locals and tourists alike.

Whether or not Ben was a lost cause wasn't the only thing on her mind. Diving was her livelihood. It was a dangerous hobby, a dangerous passion, and as one of the most respected guides on Whidbey Island, she took her reputation, and her gear, seriously.

It was her duty to find this guy.

She continued the search, ascending ten feet and scanning another 360 in all directions.

No bubbles.

No Ben.

She could feel herself using more oxygen than she should, despite her efforts to stay calm.

And then the water around her began to stir, a subtle shift in the currents signaling the end of the slack tide. The calm waters would soon be gone. She glanced at her dive computer—the oxygen level in her tank was approaching the reserve mark. She was using too much oxygen.

Time to surface.

Carla continued her slow ascent, pausing for safety stops and watching the colorful undersea world disappear, still scanning for signs of life. The environment was surreal, with rocky formations jutting out like ancient monoliths, their crevices adorned with vibrant anemones. The kelp forest above cast dappled shadows, creating an almost hypnotic dance of light and dark.

Pausing about fifteen feet below the surface, her eye caught a play of light filtering through the water. Then she saw it—a shape, vaguely human, lying against a rocky outcrop.

She studied it, the swaying kelp letting odd patterns of light and shadow play with the form, and her mind.

For some reason it made her think of her father. Maybe she wished it were her father, left lifeless and subject to the whims of the tides.

Ben!

She swam fiercely against the current and, gradually, the shape came into focus. A wrinkled face eerily distorted by the water. Carla's breath hitched in her regulator.

Fish had nibbled away at its features, leaving it hauntingly skeletal. But from what she could tell, it was certainly not Ben. The man was at least as old as her father would be now, possibly much older.

Fear gripped her as she struggled to process the horrific sight. With the change in tide and her low oxygen, she knew she would be struggling to reach the surface, even without dragging this lifeless body along with her.

She had to leave it.

She fought the rising panic, her professional instincts urging her to remain calm. But the terror was overwhelming. She turned to swim away, accidentally flicking one of the body's stray limbs with a fin.

Giving a final, terrified glance at the lifeless form over her shoulder, Carla let the tide pull her away from the corpse as she kicked frantically towards the surface.

CHAPTER TWO

Silverdale, Washington

Tuesday

THOMAS AUSTIN DRUMMED his fingertips on the table, rifling through a stack of cold cases that his boss Lucy had assigned him to look over. His first week as a detective for the Kitsap County Sheriff's Department had been as exciting as watching paint dry.

Despite the fact that some categories of property crime were up in the county—porch thefts and car burglaries, for example—the types of violent crimes he and the other detectives of the Kitsap Sheriff's Department investigated had been in decline.

That was a good thing, of course, but it had led to a fairly slow week.

Not that he minded. It was 8 AM on the Tuesday of his second week, and he was supposed to find a cold case he could crack in this stack of papers. He intended to do just that.

The four cases he'd read through that morning had piqued his interest in various ways, but none had given him clear direction. In a case from two years ago, a pizza parlor owner had vanished without a trace, leaving behind a struggling family and a trail that went cold quickly when his car was found abandoned with no signs of foul play. In the second, a series of arson incidents had plagued a quiet neighborhood in Poulsbo, with the most recent fire occurring six months ago and the case stalling due to a lack of witnesses or physical evidence.

The third case was the body of a eighty-five-year-old man found on the shore near the Manette Bridge near Bremerton, a case with few leads and no immediate suspects. The detectives assigned to the case, working closely with the medical examiner, had ruled the death an accidental drowning due to the man's history of wandering away from his apartment.

The fourth case involved a young woman who had disappeared after a night out in Silverdale, her last known location a dive bar near the waterfront. The investigation hit a dead end when surveillance footage from the area proved inconclusive.

Austin was about to dig into the next case when he heard Kendall Shaw's voice from the hallway. "Jimmy," she was saying, "you truly look like hell warmed over. You look like you woke up on the floor of a sports bar after your team lost the Super Bowl and you shotgunned twenty beers to get over the pain."

Austin heard Jimmy's laugh from the hallway. "We can't all be model-thin and well-dressed like you, Kendall. Some of us never escaped to L.A. to learn about fashion and smoothies and whatever else you did down there."

Kendall chuckled as she came through the door, followed by Jimmy and then Lucy, who had recently become lead detective in the Kitsap County Sheriff's Office when their former boss, Ridley Calvin, had been elected governor.

Kendall was right. Jimmy looked tired and a bit disheveled, and Austin knew why.

He'd been sleeping on the couch for over a week after making what he thought was a wonderful gesture: offering to renovate the garage and turn it into a mother-in-law suite so Lucy's mom could move in. Apparently, Lucy needed a little more distance and resented the fact that Jimmy had offered this to her mother without consulting her first. Austin took it as a lesson: unless you want to sleep on the couch, never set your wife up to be her mother's bad guy.

Their morning meetings usually began with some banter between Lucy and Jimmy. It was so common, Austin noticed himself waiting for her to make fun of his meathead appearance and large muscles, which Austin knew she actually loved, and him to come up with various iterations of her nickname, Lucy O-Lemonade, Lucy O-Lovehandles, and so on.

But this morning, there was no banter. Lucy stood at the whiteboard and Jimmy sat in the back, not even around the cheap folding tables. Kendall sat next to Austin, the black leather of her jacket crinkling as she settled in. He could smell the leather polish she'd applied, which deepened its rich, high-end sheen.

He and Kendall had gotten off to a bit of a rocky start, but ended up working well together despite their different styles, both in personality and law enforcement. The one thing they did have in common was that they both had corgis; Austin's Pembroke and Kendall's Cardigan Welsh got along famously. She had taken some time off after learning they had inadvertently nabbed the man who had killed her mother. But now she was back, and as much as Austin wouldn't want to admit it, he was looking forward to working with her again.

Lucy cleared her throat. "I know I told you two to be working on cold cases, and we still need to do that, but we've just gotten a call."

"Something to get us out of the office?" Kendall asked.

"Something that will get Jimmy and me out of the office," Lucy countered, "but not you two. Larsen is still all over us."

"Who?" Kendall asked.

"You know, Marty Larsen. He's only our *County Commissioner...*" Apparently Jimmy wasn't the only one Lucy planned to take her frustration out on. The rest of the team would be suffering her wrath as well.

"Right, right," Kendall said. "We call him Marsen, pronounced *Martian*. Because that guy seems like he must be from another planet."

"We were gonna nickname him *Mar-Lar*," Jimmy added, "but that was too hard to say."

Marty Larsen was a member of the Kitsap County Board of Commissioners from District 2. A smarmy, Napoleon-type guy, he was small, loud, and mean. Lately, he'd been using the sheriff's department, and specifically the hiring of Austin himself, as political fodder in an upcoming special election. He objected to the hiring of Austin, citing declining violent crime statistics and saying that the money could be better spent elsewhere. It was thanks to him that Austin had been digging through cold cases like a starving man digging through a trash can looking for morsels of sustenance. Lucy had warned Austin that they needed to put a win on the board sooner rather than later, or things could get messy.

"Anyway," Lucy said, "we got a call from the Island County Sheriff. Derby. I think it's Will Derby or maybe Willie or Bill, or well, I don't actually know what to call him, but let's just call him Derby. We—"

"That's a county over," Jimmy said.

Lucy offered up a chilling side-eye. "That's right Jimmy," her voice had a condescending lilt to it, as if she were speaking to a three-year-old. "That's why I said *Island County*. Are we in Island County, Jimmy?"

Jimmy said nothing.

"What does he want our help with?" Austin asked, trying to cut the tension.

"We've got the USRV," Lucy said.

"RV what?" asked Jimmy. His voice reminded Austin of a puppy hoping to get a treat.

"Underwater Search and Rescue Volunteers." Lucy's voice was curt and she didn't return Jimmy's eye contact. "They are excellent, and he wants to know if he can borrow them. They haven't actually pulled the body up yet, but they know it's there."

Austin shook his head. "A jumper?"

"Could be," Lucy said. "We really don't know."

"Wait a second," Austin said. "*Underwater* Rescue? How do they know they have a body down there if they don't have eyes on it yet?"

"He didn't want to say much," Lucy said, pacing in front of the whiteboard. "He was a little cagey about it, in fact. Probably just territorial."

"So he wanted our help," Jimmy said, "but *didn't* want to share the full story?"

Lucy ignored him. "The plan for the day is the follow-ing: Austin and Kendall, you two are going to stay here and work those cold cases. *Jimmy* and I—" she said his name with a hint of derision—"will connect with the USRV team and drive out to Island County."

"Can I make a case for me and Austin?" Kendall asked, standing.

Austin was surprised; he had resigned himself to sitting inside all day reading old case files.

Lucy cocked her head, frowning, but finally nodded.

Kendall said, "I've got a diving background."

Lucy raised an eyebrow.

"Well," Kendall corrected, "I dove a few times. Once, actually. But lemme me talk to the team. I can speak their language."

"It's not like we need to speak their language to ask them to go dive for a body. They've done this before. Unless you're planning to strap on a snorkel..."

"Come on, boss," Kendall implored. "I'm back from two weeks in L.A. and the sun is out in Kitsap, for *once*. Please, for the love of all that is good and holy, let Austin and me go out there and get some rays. Looking at these old cases is making me cross eyed."

Austin hadn't been planning to push it, but Kendall had made a solid case, and getting out of the office sure sounded good. "I hear that Sheriff Derby is fairly new over there as well," he said. "Maybe he and I could connect on being the new guy. Wouldn't hurt us to have a good relationship with him. Plus..." Austin was ready to twist the screw... "do you really want to spend an hour or two in the car with Jimmy?"

"Hey," Jimmy protested, shooting a glare. "That was a low blow."

Austin shrugged.

"Come to think of it..." Lucy said.

"An hour or two *each way*," Austin added, hoping that would be the final nail.

Lucy looked from Austin to Jimmy, then to Kendall. "Fine, but call us with an update as soon as you speak with Derby, and Kendall, try not to be too condescending to the dive team. They know what they're doing."

CHAPTER THREE

THE WARM MAY sun was already high in the sky as Austin and Kendall drove out of Silverdale. Pine trees flanked the highway, and Austin cracked the window to allow their fresh scent to fill the car along with the salty tang of the nearby Sound. As he drove, the landscape flickered by—a green blur punctuated by the occasional house or barn.

"You mind the radio?" Kendall asked, reaching for the dial.

"Go for it," Austin said.

She turned on a rock station and the car filled with a hard rock song Austin wasn't familiar with. He didn't like it much, but didn't mind it much either. The song faded out and an ethereal atmospheric soundscape filled the car. The sound of a faint clock ticking built up in layers, joined by bells and alarm clock ringing before the chaos became organized under rhythmic guitar and bass riffs.

"My mom used to play this song," Kendall said. "*Time*, it's called. Do you like Pink Floyd?"

"Oh, we've never met," Austin quipped.

Kendall groaned and then turned the volume up and they listened to the song.

Austin put the car on cruise control at seventy, letting the haunting chords wash over him, each note resonating with the passage of years he'd sometimes cherished, other times endured. He focused in on the words.

You find ten years have got behind you

No one told you when to run, you missed the starting gun

The lyrics stirred memories—Fiona, his time in the NYPD, his recent spate of cases and, most of all, the relentless march of time.

Kendall turned the radio down when the song ended and the station switched to advertisements. "When you're little," she said, "your parents are just your parents. You don't think about it much. And there's absolutely no way to appreciate what *they're* going through because *you're* going through the hard task of growing up."

Austin took the turn onto the Hood Canal Bridge, which would take them toward Port Townsend and, eventually, the ferry. He didn't reply, just turned off the radio completely. He could tell Kendall had more to say.

"I saw a meme on Facebook the other day. It said something about how when we are kids, we're unaware that we're also watching our parents grow up. I don't think I could have gotten that until recently. I changed so much between twenty-five and thirty-five. I mean, I am a woman in law enforcement, I have to throw my weight around to be heard and respected. But I wouldn't even recognize the shallow, self-centered, egotistical bitch I was back then."

She cast a look at Austin, which he interpreted as a cue not to say anything.

"Yeah, I *know*," she continued. "I'm *still* like that sometimes." She laughed. "You think I'm bad now, you should have seen me back then. After finding out that my mom didn't take her own life, that she struggled with depression and the horrors of this world, but kept going... I don't know. It changed me. You ever think about having kids?"

"Think about it? Yeah. But never really got close. Fiona and I... well.. Maybe I missed the starting gun."

"From the song, right?" Kendall laughed. "I didn't think you were listening."

"I was. Fiona and I were always too committed to our jobs and now, well, it's probably too late."

"It's not too late," Kendall said. "It's never too late."

Austin wasn't sure if she was talking about him, or about herself. "What about you? How long do you plan on kicking around on a piece of ground in your home town?"

"Clever," Kendall said, smiling. "You really were listening. There was a huge paradigm shift for me when I learned about my mom. Before that I would never have even considered having children. Now, I don't know. Not that I'm dating. I mean, the first case we worked together kind of scared me away from the dating apps."

Austin could understand. The case had involved a murderer finding his victims through a dating app for seniors. "That makes sense. How's your dad doing with it all?"

"He's good," Kendall said. "I had been so worried about him, but the relief he felt and the closure he got when I told him about mom changed him. He's very religious—in his paradigm victims of suicide go to hell. He's found peace in knowing that someday he'll see my mother again, where before he'd been heartbroken to think that they wouldn't be reunited in Heaven. When I see him he always says, *'Now, I can die with a smile on my face.'*"

"I'm glad for him," Austin said.

"Me too." Kendall sighed deeply. "How's *your* dad, by the way?"

"Just okay, I think. My dad and mom recently moved back to the area. They've got him in a great memory care facility in Seattle, at least for now. Evergreen, it's called. My mom's living in a hotel nearby while they figure out their next move. I feel like I should be doing more for them but my mother just tells me to focus on myself and that she wants me to find happiness."

He swallowed hard. His voice was optimistic, but each time he spoke about it, a sadness descended. They were all doing the best they could, but nothing could make the situation feel anything more than adequate.

"I guess we're just at that age," Kendall said. "That age where we spend as much time worrying about our parents as they used to spend worrying about us. You do enough, Austin."

"Maybe. My mother is always quoting some line about our children being our hearts walking around outside of our bodies. I can't really relate."

"Sure you can relate," Kendall said. "How do you feel when Run is happy?"

"Happy, I guess," Austin agreed.

"And when she's sad or in pain?" Kendall asked. "You want to comfort her right? And when she feels better, you do, too."

"You're right," he had to admit.

"The same is true for me and Ralph."

She smiled sadly, then turned the radio back on. *American Girl* by Tom Petty and the Heartbreakers filled the car. The song was a fast-moving, hard rocking jam—less introspective, maybe, but much more fun.

Exactly what they needed to lighten the mood.

~

At the Port Townsend ferry terminal, Austin maneuvered the car into line, his eyes scanning the busy dock. The ferry bobbed gently at its moorings. Once on board, they got out of the car and stood at the rail, the deck vibrating under them as the ferry's engines rumbled to life. They stood in silence as the town shrank behind them, replaced by the long stretch of blue water.

The crossing was smooth, the sea like glass under the bright sky. Reaching Coupeville, Austin drove off the ferry and headed north. As they crossed the Deception Pass Bridge, its iron spans stark against the blue sky, the water below churned with the tide.

Austin parked in a small turnaround area along the side of the road, and, as he stepped out of the car, only the knowledge of what the team of volunteers was in the process of diving for could darken the otherwise stunning day.

Every direction was like a different postcard—water and trees, little white boats, rocky and sandy shores, and clouds as big, billowy, and white as a cartoon.

Seeing a dive team member on the shore, Austin's mood went somber, locking into the fact that they were there to watch a body be pulled from those picturesque waters.

As he closed the door to the car, he heard a voice behind him. "Detectives Austin and Shaw?"

He turned to see the outstretched hand of Sheriff Derby.

Austin accepted his hand and shook it. "I'm Austin, Detective Austin these days, and this is Detective Kendall Shaw." It was the first time in years he'd introduced himself as 'Detective Austin.'

Derby was a black man in his early fifties, with closely cropped hair that was beginning to gray at the temples. He wore thin, rectangular glasses that gave him a studious look, and his eyes moved slowly, but seemed to bore deep into the object of their focus when they landed on something. "Lucy called and said you two were on your way," he said. "Your dive team beat you here, and I sure appreciate the help. Plenty of great divers in Island County, of course, but we're a smaller community and don't have a team affiliated with law enforcement." He took off his glasses and cleaned them on his shirt before putting them back on with a sigh. "They've been down there for about five minutes." He nodded down the slope, and they began walking toward the water.

"May I ask," Kendall said, "how did you get the tip about the body?"

Derby frowned, his forehead creasing. "It came in as an anonymous tip. Sort of anonymous, anyway."

"Sort of?" Kendall asked.

"Long story," Derby said.

"And one I hope we can return to," Austin said. "But how far down was the body?"

"Caller didn't say, but..." Derby pointed toward the surface of the water, where a diver had just emerged. "Maybe not all that deep. They haven't been down there long."

They stopped about ten yards from the shore, watching as the team of volunteers emerged from the waters beneath Deception Pass Bridge. Together, the three divers moved efficiently, lifting a body out of the water and carrying it over the rocks and onto a patch of bright green grass.

Derby nodded toward the body and the divers backed away. "Here's the part I hate."

He led them closer and Austin found himself standing over the body of a man who looked at least ninety years old, clad in a long coat. The sight was unsettling and Austin had to look away momentarily to steel his stomach, and his nerves. The man had pale white skin marked with several dark moles, and his features had been partially eaten away by fish or crabs, leaving a haunting, skeletal visage.

The divers communicated quietly, their expressions grim but professional as they handled the body with care. The coat, now waterlogged and tattered, clung to the man's frail form.

"This is horrible," Kendall said. "But, for me, telling the family is always the worst part. Any family found yet?"

Derby didn't reply. After a long silence, he said, "We will get the full medical examination, but I'm going to make a quick inspection." He put on nitrile gloves and reached toward one of the pockets of the coat, which Austin now saw was a dark brown knee-length raincoat. "I'm no ME, but he was in the water for a while, at least a few days."

"Agreed," Austin said. "Maybe a week."

"No immediate signs of bruising or other injuries," Derby said, "but we won't know for sure until we get the full report."

Crouching, Derby pulled a handful of medium-sized gray and blue stones from inside the pocket of the man's coat, the kind one might use on a garden path or driveway. "He was weighed down," Derby said. "That's murder."

"Possibly," Kendall said. "Or suicide."

Either was definitely possible with the little information they had, Austin thought, but there were other options as well. "My dad has dementia and has a habit of filling his pockets with stuff. First week in his new facility over in Seattle, he put a small clock radio in his pocket along with all the change he could find, someone else's hearing aid, and three pairs of socks. He wandered out of the facility. They stopped him in the parking lot."

"What are you saying?" Kendall asked.

Austin crouched to examine the man's bare feet, which

were missing a total of three toes. "I guess I'm wondering whether there's any chance this was a tragic accident."

"If this guy had dementia," Derby countered, "how could he have made it to the bridge? No facilities within walking distance. Plus, already checked, and no local facilities are missing anyone."

"Anyone else reported missing?" Kendall asked. "Maybe the family reported it."

Derby shook his head as he leaned in toward the man's face. "No one that matches the description." He put the rocks back in the man's pocket.

"Are those rocks even enough to weigh down a body?" Austin asked.

Kendall said, "The buoyancy of the human body is fairly close to that of water. To make a man like this sink, you only need fifteen or twenty pounds of extra weight."

Derby examined the other pocket. "Pockets are deep, and full. I'm guessing this is fifteen to twenty pounds. No way an old man stuffed that in his own pockets and took a header off the bridge by accident. And no way he gets out here without a car on his own. Someone was hiding this body or disposing of it."

Austin nodded. "Is there anything else you can tell us about the anonymous tip?"

Derby shoved his hands in his pockets. "*Can* tell you or *will* tell you?"

Austin realized he had overstepped. "I know this isn't our case. We're only here to provide the divers. I'm just curious, that's all."

"It was a priest," Derby said matter-of-factly.

Kendall glanced at Austin, probably thinking the same thing he was. "Did the priest say how he knew about the body?"

"Said he heard about it from someone in his parish."

Austin cocked his head. "A parishioner confessed to his priest? That indicates a lot of guilt. Potential suspect?"

Derby nodded up the slope to where the medical examination team had parked and was making its way down. "Maybe," he said. "But for now, we need a cause of death. And we need to find out who this guy is. Maybe that will tell us why he ended up on the rocks at the bottom of the strait under Deception Pass bridge."

Kendall gestured up the slope to the car. "And we need to get back to the office."

CHAPTER FOUR

AUSTIN GRIPPED the steering wheel tight, anger rising from his chest to his face as he looked across the parking lot of the Kitsap County Sheriff's Department. It was never a good day when TV news cameras were around. Usually, it meant they had a high-profile case—a gruesome murder or something like that.

Today it was because the Martian was there—County Commissioner Marty Larsen.

Getting out of the car, Austin exchanged a look with Kendall and followed her across the parking lot, stopping about five yards from the pontificating politician.

"Not only," Larsen was saying, "did this department spend more money last quarter than every previous quarter on record, they hired a *new* detective. A former *New Yorker*, at that. And what did they spend their day doing today, this crack team of ace detectives? They spent it over in Island County, assisting with a case not even in their jurisdiction. Now, I support law enforcement as much as anyone else. After all, my father and uncles were all state troopers. But violent crime is *down* in this county, our infrastructure is in desperate need of repair, and we shouldn't be diverting much-needed resources from those projects, not to mention other important departments, to pay for this bloated squad."

There were only three or four reporters and one cameraman watching the press conference, and Austin was happy that none of them were local reporter Anna Downey. He and Anna had worked closely together on a few cases when he first became involved as a consultant with the Kitsap Sheriff's Department. Later, they had dated briefly.

A massive betrayal on Anna's part had ended the relationship, and lately they had only exchanged occasional, polite text messages. He was happy that she wasn't there because, even though he did not have any residual animosity toward her, it was still awkward.

He was surprised to hear her voice behind him the moment Larsen stopped speaking. Apparently she had emerged from inside the office.

"Commissioner Larsen," she asked, walking between Austin and Kendall, "isn't it the case that last year you voted for thirty percent salary increases for yourself and the other county commissioners while police officers received only a six percent raise?"

Austin smiled. One thing he had liked about Anna was that she didn't fear confrontation with sources.

"I, we, I mean they, I mean we..." Larsen was stammering. "Yes, that was what was passed, however—"

Anna cut him off. "And isn't it the case that, since Governor Ridley left the role of lead detective and the position of Sheriff is temporarily vacant, this quarter's expenses are actually projected to be *lower* than second quarter last year, even with the addition of Detective Austin?"

"Well, um, perhaps," Larsen managed to say before Anna continued.

"And isn't it *also* the case that the Kitsap County Sheriff's Department operates on a lower budget than most
similarly sized departments in Washington?"

Austin didn't need to wait for the reply. All of the politics and BS made for good blog posts and TV news broad-
casts and podcasts and whatever other media Anna had her
hands on these days, but it didn't affect him. He figured
that, if they eventually cut his position out of the budget,
there was nothing he could do about it.

For now, he had work to do.

Inside, Kendall and Austin met Lucy and Jimmy in the little
conference room, which smelled of stale coffee and the
fresh coat of white paint he and Jimmy had applied over the
weekend.

"Still no ID on the body," Lucy said as they walked in,
"and we've got to pivot from this thing soon since it's not
our case, but Derby *did* send over the preliminary ME
report. In case we were curious."

Samantha, the department's technical analyst, sauntered
in holding a laptop under each arm. Austin hadn't seen her
in a while and, apparently, she'd used her time off to get a
new tattoo. It appeared to be a red, white, and blue shield
with a star on the back of her right hand.

Austin wasn't sure what it was about young people and
their tattoos. He wasn't really for it or against it; all he
knew was that it made him feel old.

Samantha held up her hand, showing off the new tattoo.

No one said anything.

"Hellooooo?" she said. "You don't recognize it?"

Silence.

"It's Captain America's shield."

Austin nodded, even though it still didn't mean much to him.

"How was your honeymoon?" Jimmy asked her.

"Great," Samantha said. "We watched every movie in the Marvel cinematic universe in order, then got matching tattoos."

Jimmy offered an odd smile, as though he was about to make a sarcastic comment, but he bit his lip. He and Samantha were polar opposites, but that didn't seem to stop them from working well together. Samantha plugged one of the laptops into a long black cord, and the screen on the wall lit up.

"This just came in," she said.

Preliminary Medical Examiner's Report

Date: *May 22, 2024*
Case Number: *C2887*
Name: *John Doe*
Location: *Deception Pass Bridge, Island County*
Description of Decedent:

- *Age: 95-100 years*
- *Height: 5 ft 8 in*
- *Weight: 160 lbs*
- *Identifying Marks: A small, faded tattoo of the letters "CB" with an anchor intertwined on his right ankle.*
- *Dental Records: No matches.*
- *Clothing: Brown slacks, white t-shirt, dark brown, knee-length raincoat*

External Examination: *The body exhibits signs of prolonged submersion in water. The face and extremities show significant postmortem damage, likely caused by aquatic scavengers.*

On examination, no visible signs of trauma, such as lacerations or bruising, were observed.

Initial Brain Scan: *The brain scan reveals several key indicators of dementia. There is noticeable cortical atrophy, particularly in the hippocampus and frontal lobe, regions critical for memory and executive function. The ventricles appear enlarged, a sign of brain shrinkage. Additionally, there are hyperintensities in the white matter, which could suggest chronic small vessel disease, commonly associated with aging and dementia.*

Internal Examination: *Preliminary autopsy findings are inconclusive regarding the cause of death. Lung examination revealed the presence of fluid, consistent with drowning. However, due to the advanced state of decomposition and the absence of definitive signs of struggle or injury, it is not possible to conclusively determine if the individual drowned or if the fluid accumulation occurred postmortem.*

Toxicology: *Pending*

Conclusion: *At this stage, the evidence is insufficient to definitively classify the manner of death. Further investigation and analysis, including toxicology and potential identification through familial DNA, are required to determine whether the decedent died from drowning or was deceased prior to submersion.*

When they'd all finished reading, Lucy said, "We still don't know much about this fellow and Derby assured me he'd take it from here, but—"

"His tattoo," Austin said. "Samantha, can you pull up anything about the Navy's CBs? It might be spelled *C-B* or it could be *Seabee*, like the body of water and the bug that makes honey."

Samantha chuckled but, when she saw the serious look on Austin's face, she began typing.

"What is it?" Kendall asked.

"He's a veteran," Austin said. "Navy. World War Two. CB stands for *Construction Battalion* and their nickname was the Seabees. Means he's *at least* 95 years old, probably 100. He may have lied about his age to get into the war."

Samantha read from a report she'd quickly pulled up online. "Formed during World War II, the *Seabees* (a phonetic spelling of "CB" for Construction Battalion) were created to meet the need for skilled construction workers who could also defend themselves. They were responsible for building airstrips, roads, bridges, and other crucial infrastructure in combat zones."

"Most Seabees were older," Austin said. "Already skilled in a trade. He would have been one of the youngest."

He let out a long breath. Thoughts of this man as a teenager, maybe no more than sixteen or seventeen, working construction for the Navy in World War Two, had lodged painfully in his chest. Austin tasted moldy bread, his stomach turning in disgust at this crime, assuming this was a murder, as Austin was now convinced it was. He thought too of his own father, younger than this John Doe and only twenty miles away as the crow would fly, but, because of his condition, he felt much further away than that.

"So we've got a man around ninety-five or a hundred years old," Kendall said. "A World War Two veteran. And we have three options. First, he was killed and someone dumped his body over the bridge, or dropped him in the water from the shore, weighed down with rocks to make sure he sank. Second, that he wandered away from somewhere and fell accidentally, though I still don't see how that could have worked. And finally..."

She trailed off. She didn't want to say it, and neither did Austin.

"Hate to say it," Jimmy said, his voice low, and less upbeat than Austin usually heard from the gregarious

Jimmy. "Suicide. Can't be ruled out. Deaths of despair are on the rise."

Austin looked at the table, something inside him twisting.

After a long silence, Lucy cleared her throat. "The veteran angle might help us find records," she said, walking to the door of the conference room. "I've got to meet with that Larsen bastard about the budget, then I'll give Sheriff Derby a call to let him know what we've learned about our John Doe."

CHAPTER FIVE

LUCY CAME BACK into the conference room about twenty minutes later. "They narrowed it down to three churches," she said. "Where the priest who made the tip works." Just then, her phone buzzed in her pocket and she excused herself to take the call, promising to be back in a minute to explain everything.

While she had been on the phone with Derby and meeting with Larsen, Austin had felt his mood sour even further.

He had gone through multiple phases in his life during which he'd been obsessed with World War Two history. He'd read books, watched documentaries, and watched feature films as well. The thought of any ninety-five or hundred year old man taking his own life by leaping off a picturesque bridge that connected wealthy and beautiful communities was unbelievably tragic. Add in the fact that he'd been a veteran of World War Two and somehow that made the whole thing even sadder.

And that was just one possibility. Murder, Austin

thought, was still most likely. But why a man with dementia who was already so near the end?

Austin tried not to allow himself to wallow, but there was something about this one that brought a darkness over him that he couldn't push away easily.

When Lucy returned, she said, "There are dozens of churches in Island County, but only three Catholic churches. Derby said that some of the background noise—some particular song—indicated to him that it was one of the Catholic churches."

"Assuming they eventually locate the priest who made the call, is the priest himself a suspect?" Jimmy asked. "I mean, he's the one who knew about the location of the body."

Lucy shook her head. "Derby said he wasn't, but who knows? He was cagey. Obviously, he wants this case to himself."

"And have they identified the body yet?" Kendall asked.

"No," Lucy said. "I told him about the tattoo, and they were already checking Naval records. So far, nothing. No fingerprints either. Too decomposed. They checked missing person reports from the whole state. Nothing that matches our John Doe. No matching dental records have turned up yet, either."

Austin placed his hands flat on the table. Of course, he wanted to dig into this one further, but he knew it wasn't in the cards.

"The guy is a complete mystery," Lucy said, "and we need to get back to work on our own cases. The Martian is on the warpath."

~

Hello. You have reached the voicemail of Simone Aoki. Please leave a message after the tone.

Austin ended the call and shoved his phone back in his pocket.

Crouching, he picked up a little rubber frisbee and tossed it down the beach. It hit a patch of wind and blew about six feet into the shallow water. Run, his corgi, raced after it, but paused at the edge of the water and glanced back at Austin.

"You can do it," Austin said. "You swim, remember?"

He shook his head, smiling. Run was smart and athletic. She knew how to swim, and Austin had seen her dive enthusiastically into this water many times. He *knew* she could get the frisbee, but she preferred not to and was looking at him to find out if he could be convinced.

He waved toward the frisbee. "Get it," he said. "Get your frisbee."

Run gave him one more glance and waded into the water as though testing it for temperature. Then she dove in fully and paddled out to the frisbee, grabbing it between her teeth before turning around and paddling back. When she hit the beach, she shook herself off violently, then sprinted up to Austin, stopping in front of him with a sandy skid and dropping the frisbee.

"Great job," he said. "But you really are turning into a diva."

He tossed the frisbee again, this time not so hard and not so far, making sure it would land in the sand, which Run preferred.

Austin and Sy had been playing phone tag for days. They'd exchanged a few texts, mostly trying unsuccessfully to set up a time to speak, which Austin still preferred when possible.

He tossed the frisbee again, watching a small sailboat pass about a quarter mile out into the Sound.

There was something in the sound of Simone's voice that soothed him. A calm, he thought, a maturity earned by getting through difficult times. Like him, she had been through a lot. A law enforcement career. The death of a spouse. He wasn't sure exactly where things were headed, but he knew they were getting fairly serious. He wasn't sure what her next move would be, but he hoped it would start with a move to Washington State.

Right now, he wanted to speak with her about the deceased man they'd found under Deception Pass Bridge. Even though it wasn't his case, it was sticking with him like it was.

His phone buzzed in his pocket, and he pulled it out. A text from Simone.

Just got through meeting with the board. Looks like my early retirement is going to be approved. Can't talk now, I have a doctor appointment. Talk tonight or maybe tomorrow?

Austin gave the message a thumbs-up emoji, something he had just learned to do, which always made him feel a little bit lazy, so he went ahead and tapped out a reply as Run waited patiently, catching her breath in the sand. "Congratulations, Sy. I knew they would approve. And yes, TTYS."

Austin had learned *TTYS* only recently from a text he'd received from her. At first he'd thought she'd had a stroke while texting him, then she'd explained it meant Talk To You Soon.

Austin picked up the frisbee. He noticed that Run was still panting and decided they should head back. His corgi would play past the point of complete exhaustion, and Austin had read online that, with corgis, you sometimes need to stop them because they won't stop themselves from overexertion.

As the sun set, he walked slowly down the beach, enjoying the night air. It was cool but not cold, and he was looking forward to a hot summer of beach days, maybe some fishing, and a cold beer or two at his little café, general store, and bait shop.

But even all of those lovely thoughts couldn't lighten his mood.

The Pink Floyd song had stuck with him, causing endless circular thoughts about the fact that his dad, finally living close by, could no longer communicate with him for more than a few minutes a day. And as sad as that was, at least he had Austin's mom to take care of him, not to mention the caregivers at what was an excellent memory care facility.

The John Doe, Austin thought, had none of that.

They still hadn't found any evidence that anyone was looking for the man. And it made him wonder, wasn't someone in charge of looking after people who didn't have family, didn't have friends? How was it possible that a veteran around a hundred years old could wind up in the water under the bridge and not a single person had reported him missing?

CHAPTER SIX

Wednesday

THE NEXT MORNING, Austin was back on the beach with Run, repeating the ritual of throwing and retrieving that they'd performed the night before. This time, they were using a stick instead of a frisbee.

It was 7 AM sharp, so he called his mom. She had told him that was the hour during which she always visited his dad and the hour during which his dad was most likely to be lucid. "Hey, Mom," he said, "how is he today?"

"Not great," she replied. "Not a good time to talk with him, I'm afraid. Today he called me Sally, his sister's name. Asked if I was still dating Mike Dexter."

She let out a long sigh and Austin could almost feel the weight of her concern, her sadness.

"What did you tell him?" he asked.

"What *could* I tell him? I played along. I told him I was thinking of marrying the guy."

"You did not," Austin said, chuckling.

His mom always knew how to bring a little levity into dark situations.

"I did, and it made him smile. He still has his smile."

"And everybody loves the thought of a wedding."

"Some days I just don't know, Thomas." Hearing his mother say his first name always brought him the feeling of home and safety. Only his parents still called him that.

"I'm going to come over this weekend," Austin said, crouching to pick up the stick before launching it down the beach.

"Good," his mother said. "That's good. And how are things going with Simone? You know, I had a feeling about her the second you told me you two were dating."

Austin recalled all too well. His mother had found a photo of Sy online within five minutes of Austin mentioning her name, and had probably started crocheting a sweater for her imaginary grandkids five minutes later. "You would have had a feeling about a lump of clay if you thought I might be able to use it to sculpt some grandbabies for you."

"It's not my fault," she said. "I can't help but long for the grandkids you two might give me. And your father, of course."

Austin shoved a hand in his pocket, the other holding his phone close to his ear. The beach was deserted, which was another reason Austin liked to walk early in the morning or late at night. Technically, he was supposed to have Run on a leash, but he had one at the ready in case another dog appeared. But usually on this stretch, there was no one around unless it was midday or a sunny weekend.

"You sound down," his mom said.

"It's a case," Austin said. "Not even *my* case. World War Two vet found under a bridge. Drowned. Possibly murdered. Could be suicide."

"Oh my God," his mother said. "That's terrible. A World War Two veteran, you said? Not a lot of them are still with us, sadly."

"I know," Austin said. "He's probably in his late nineties."

"You don't know how old he is?"

"We don't have an ID on the body," Austin said.

Run dropped the stick on Austin's foot, and something clicked in his mind. A file from the other day and a photo of another elderly body on a beach, this one next to a few driftwood sticks.

His mother had changed the topic and was lecturing him about not giving her any grandchildren. Run was staring up at him politely, occasionally letting out a little quiet bark, indicating that it was again time to throw the stick.

If he was remembering correctly, the man found dead near the Manette Bridge in Bremerton had not been immediately identified either. He had no living family and there had been no initial report of his disappearance. Another similarity to the man found a couple days before was that the Bremerton man showed early signs of dementia.

It wasn't much, but it was a connection. At the very least, it might be enough to get Lucy to agree to put him and Kendall on the case, since the Manette Bridge death had taken place in Kitsap County.

He tuned back in as his mother finished her lecture. "I know you want grandkids, mom, and you'd make the best grandmother. I'm just not sure I'm fatherhood material."

"I thought that bringing Fiona's case to a close would free you up emotionally," his mother said. "Anyway, grandkids aside, tell me, what is going on with Sy? You said she might be moving out there."

"These days it's hard for us even to connect on a phone

call," Austin said. "But yeah, maybe. It's all... we don't know, it's complicated. I'll give you a call tomorrow. I have to get into the office."

Austin pointed at a printed color photograph that he'd taped to the whiteboard in the conference room, the man who'd been found deceased near the Manette Bridge. His body was mostly covered by a white cloth. "Hank Butterfield. He was the deceased in one of the cold cases I was looking through the other day. Very few details on the case because, at the time, it was deemed to be an accidental drowning. He was eighty-five years old and still living on his own in a studio apartment in a house that had been converted into four units. Butterfield had early signs of dementia, and his landlord had even petitioned with county authorities to have him placed in a home because he had stopped paying rent and had wandered out of his apartment a couple times. His case was pending at the time of his death, which went unnoticed for forty-eight hours."

Austin looked up at Kendall, who sat in her leather jacket, arms folded, studying the whiteboard. Jimmy and Lucy sat on opposite ends of the table, each sipping coffee. Apparently, the iceberg between them had thawed somewhat because, at least, they'd come in together that morning.

He had called the meeting, but felt a little odd standing in Lucy's spot at the whiteboard. Previously, this had been Ridley Calvin's spot but, since his election as governor, they saw Ridley mostly on television or on the front pages of newspapers.

Kendall tapped a pen on the table. "Any clear connection to the Manette Bridge case, Hank Butterfield, and the John Doe at Deception Pass Bridge?"

"From the original file, not much," Austin admitted. "Obviously, both men are older, and both had dementia. Plus, assuming we are right that John Doe had neither close friends or relatives to report him missing, that would be another connection."

"Who found Mr. Butterfield's body?" Lucy asked.

Austin shook his head, frowning. "School field trip. Seventh-grade marine biology class from a nearby private school. They were doing some beachcombing or something and, well..." Austin shook his head, trying to dislodge the thought of a twelve-year-old kid stumbling across Butterfield's body on the shore beneath the bridge. "There's more. Something solid. I stopped by the evidence storage facility on the way in this morning. No one ever picked up Butterfield's clothes or belongings." Austin crouched down and pulled a plastic ziplock bag filled with rocks out of his duffel bag. "He was wearing a fairly heavy wool jacket, despite being found in August. These blue and gray rocks were found in the pockets."

"They sure look a lot like the ones we found in John Doe's raincoat," Kendall said.

"Holy hell," Jimmy blurted out. "Not often you find a piece of evidence like that."

"Good work," Lucy said. "I mean, this is bleak as hell, but good work, Austin."

Kendall stood. "A serial killer?"

Austin cocked his head. "I wouldn't leap to that conclusion immediately, but we definitely have someone out there preying on the oldest, most vulnerable among us." Austin could hear the vitriol seeping through the last words he spoke. He always tried to remain cool, to stuff his emotions down while in the middle of a meeting. But this time he couldn't contain himself. "The elderly and children," he spat. "Nothing makes me angrier than people preying on the elderly and children. I don't know if this is a serial killer or something else is going on here, but I damn well want to find out." He looked up at Lucy. "Is this enough to attach ourselves to the case?"

Lucy stood, yanking out her cell phone. "Damn right it is. We have more resources than Island County, and this is enough to get them to share everything. We will have to share everything back, but I don't have any problem with that. Do you, Austin?"

Austin shook his head. "Derby seems new, but like a decent guy. Tell him we're coming over there."

"When?" Lucy said.

Austin glanced at Kendall. "Now." He shifted his gaze to Samantha, who'd been sitting silently, staring at her laptop. "Can you—"

"See if any other cases match?" she asked, not looking up from her screen. "Already on it."

"Thanks," Austin said.

Catching Kendall's eye, he hurried past her and she dropped in behind him. They needed to get back to Whidbey Island. They needed to speak with the sole person who was giving out information—the priest who'd called to notify the Island County Sheriff's department of the drowned body at Deception Pass.

Austin wanted to make sure their only fresh lead didn't spoil before he had a chance to taste it.

CHAPTER SEVEN

AUSTIN WAS ONLY HALFWAY across the parking lot when he heard Lucy's voice calling after him. "Austin, Kendall, wait," she shouted.

He turned and saw Lucy speaking into her phone and holding up a finger, indicating for them to hold on. She turned away, continuing her call, and Austin walked up just as she finished it.

"Thank you, Sheriff Da-, I mean Mr. Daniels," she said. "I know things have been, well... hello? Hello?" Lucy turned to face Austin and Kendall, frowning. "He hung up on me."

"Was that Sheriff Daniels?" Austin asked. "I mean, *former* Sheriff Daniels?"

Lucy nodded. "He got out of his second stint in rehab and sent me a text last week, said congratulations and offered to help anytime he was needed. Even said he'd support me if I wanted to run for Sheriff, assuming we get that special election at some point."

Daniels had left his role as sheriff draped in scandal, which had left Ridley Calvin running things briefly. Ridley had brought stability and professionalism to the department, but his tenure was cut short when he'd successfully run for governor, defeating Daniels in a special election.

With Ridley's departure, the sheriff's position was left vacant, leading to significant contention among the County Commissioners. Lucy had been named temporary acting sheriff, but there was no talk of her filling the role permanently. Both her young age and her lack of desire for the position made it a non-starter. The board was deadlocked, with some members advocating for an immediate appointment to ensure continued leadership, others insisting on holding a special election to allow the public to choose their new sheriff.

"Anyway," Lucy said, "I gave Daniels a quick call and he remembered the case. Butterfield. The Manette bridge drowning. I asked him if there was anything that didn't end up in the file. He said he couldn't think of anything and recalled being sure it was an accidental drowning. Not that Daniels being sure about something means much. But apparently, Butterfield was known for wandering out of his apartment at all hours of the day."

Austin shook his head. "So why did you stop us? We're hurrying for the ferry."

"Samantha found something. Another case. Similar. Also at Deception Pass Bridge."

Kendall asked, "Can she send it to my phone? We need to get going."

Lucy nodded. "You'll have it in ten minutes."

~

They hadn't even made it onto the highway by the time the report arrived from Samantha.

"Helen Virginia Fullman." Kendall read from the report as Austin drove. "Described by people she knew as a spry and active eighty-year-old. She was still driving, still living on her own and, apparently, loved to travel. Had hit every continent except for Antarctica over the ten year period before she died. She was found drowned under the Deception Pass Bridge three years ago. Before either Butterfield or our John Doe."

Austin cursed under his breath. How was it possible that there was another case at Deception Pass and that no one in the Island County Sheriff's Department had noticed the similarities? "What else do the cases have in common?"

"Just that Fullman didn't have any living family, although she seemed to have more friends than the others."

"Did she have any military experience?" Austin asked.

"No, and neither did Butterfield, so I doubt that's an angle worth pursuing. Fullman had once been married with one child, but both her husband and daughter died in a car crash in the seventies. Lived the rest of her life without getting remarried. Originally from the Green Lake neighborhood of Seattle, she moved to Kitsap in the 1980s."

"What was it that triggered Samantha on this?"

"Well, the bridge thing. Her car was found nearby, and it was deemed an accidental death. But also..." Kendall paused, letting out a sigh, "the rocks. She was found wearing a parka type jacket and was weighed down by fifteen pounds of driveway gravel. Slightly different kind, but similar enough MO that it's hard to believe it was an accident."

"Or a coincidence," Austin added. "Helen Virginia Fullman three years ago. Hank Butterfield two years ago. And John Doe a few days ago. Maybe this ends up being classified as a serial killer, or maybe something else, but either way we've now got three victims. At least."

CHAPTER EIGHT

THEY MET Sheriff Derby at a little turnout about a hundred yards from the bridge. Austin had asked Lucy to call ahead and begin laying the groundwork for sharing information between the two departments. But the stone-faced look on Derby's face as he got out of the car told Austin he might not be in the mood to play well with others.

"Let me take the lead on this," Kendall said. "Okay?"

Austin nodded. "He looks pissed," he muttered.

Seemingly ignoring them, Derby walked toward the edge of the turnout, staring down at the water a few hundred feet below. "Only been on this job for three months," he said. "County I lived in before, we didn't *have* any bridges." He shook his head.

"What county was that?" Kendall asked.

Derby turned, his arms folded, and ignored the question. "Got a call from your boss. O'Rourke. Apparently, this is part of a pattern now?" He raised an eyebrow skeptically.

"Hear us out," Kendall said. "We've got a similar case

from two years ago in Bremerton. And we just learned about Helen Virginia Fullman. Ring any bells?"

"It didn't until O'Rourke mentioned the name. Happened before my time. I'm not one to go digging into past files and questioning the work of my predecessors. Looked like an accident at the time, and that's where it still sits today."

"Come on," Austin said. "You know better than that."

Derby turned away, watching as a couple tourists took photographs of the bridge. The police tape had been removed and, as far as they knew, it was just a lovely day at a beautiful bridge. Part of Austin wished that, like them, he was ignorant about the bodies that had been sunk beneath it.

"I know, I know," Derby said. "This is not what I needed so soon after getting this job. Man I replaced is a legend, and a helluva sheriff. If he missed something it's gonna eat him up inside and make it look like I'm throwing him under the bus."

"We want to talk to the priest," Austin said. "We heard you narrowed it down to three."

Derby shook his head. "He's *our* witness. Not that we know exactly who he is yet. Department is stretched thin already and—"

"Then let us *help*," Austin said. "If someone confessed to a priest about the body, fifty-fifty chance it was our killer. Did Lucy—I mean, Detective O'Rourke—did she tell you about the stones?"

Derby nodded. "Seems pretty thin, but I guess it's enough to go on for now. Look," he let out a long sigh, "I'm already hanging on by a thread. First Black sheriff in the county's history. Don't want to upset my predecessor and I don't want to be made to look like a fool by an outside department, you know?"

Kendall glanced at Austin, telling him with her eyes that now was his time. "You have my word," Austin said. "You give us what you have, we will share everything we have with you, and hell, you can take the credit if we find anything."

"I'm not looking to take any credit," Derby said. "I just don't want to be cut out of the loop. Deal?"

Kendall reached out and shook his hand. "Deal."

"Of course," Austin added, shaking his hand.

Derby pulled a piece of paper out of his pocket and handed it to Kendall. "Those are the three churches we suspect the tip may have come from. We're doing our research on each of them before we move in. We can't take the chance that a guilty priest or parishioner gets wind of the investigation and decides to do a runner."

Without replying, Kendall turned around, and Austin watched as she snapped a photo of the list and sent it out as a text message.

Probably to Samantha, Austin thought. Kendall was more tech-savvy than Austin, and her immediate response to any new piece of evidence was to feed it to Samantha to see if she could expand on it with her digital techniques while Kendall herself looked into it on the ground. He had to admit, it was the right call, even if it wasn't one he would have thought of immediately.

Returning to the conversation, Kendall said, "Thank you, Sheriff Derby. I've got our best tech person on this now. You sent over the initial police call, correct?"

"I did," he said as his phone rang, and he excused himself to take the call, walking to the other end of the little turnout.

Cars whooshed by on the road, entering the bridge. Austin took in the scene, which was even more beautiful than the day before. The temperature must have been around seventy-two degrees, perfectly sunny, with a cool salt breeze.

That morning he'd read about the area. Named by Captain George Vancouver in 1792, Deception Pass got its name when Vancouver had passed through the treacherous, narrow strait between Whidbey Island and Fidalgo Island and realized that what he'd thought was a peninsula was actually an island.

The area's history was rich, replete with stories of the indigenous peoples who had lived there for hundreds of years and the early explorers who navigated its tricky waters. Deception Pass State Park, now a popular destination, boasted stunning views, lush forests, and a variety of wildlife, making it a place where natural beauty and history intersected. It was also a popular spot among divers, Austin had read, though the windows when it was safe to dive under the bridge were few and far between.

"Look at that," Kendall said suddenly. She was pointing at the water.

Austin glanced down but saw nothing except the gently sloshing waves. "What?"

"There was something there," Kendall said.

Austin's heart skipped a beat. He just hoped it wasn't another body. He walked forward, eyes glued to the spot she'd pointed at.

Nothing.

A large truck passed over the bridge and Austin glanced over.

"There," Kendall said. "There it was again."

He looked back at the water and saw nothing. "Are you messing with me?"

"There was something there," Kendall said. "I swear it."

Austin looked down again, staring intently at the water.

"Just keep your eyes glued," Kendall said. "Could be

another piece of clothing or a hat or something. I couldn't really see. It was dark against the dark water."

Suddenly, something popped out of the water. "Oh," Austin said. "That's a harbor seal."

The seal seemed to be looking right at them, and just as quickly as it had appeared, it disappeared. Austin watched the water move for a few seconds, and then the seal popped up again, still staring at them.

"I think he's trolling us," Kendall said. "But I'm glad it's not another... you know."

"Trolling?" Austin asked.

"It's what people say now. It means he's messing with you. He wants to get your attention for his own amusement."

"So, trolling as in using bait?"

"Right. *Cuteness* bait," Kendall said. "I want to go down and take another look at the scene, but I'm not sure if it's just because I want to get closer to that cute seal."

Austin considered this and was about to speak when Kendall held up a single finger. Her phone had vibrated in her pocket, and she pulled it out.

"Samantha is a genius," she said. "The Island County Sheriff's department has known it was one of these three churches all day, and they haven't figured out which." She turned to Austin, smiling. "It took Samantha ten minutes."

Austin looked around to make sure Derby hadn't heard her. He was still on the phone and Kendall was already hurrying back to the car.

As he jogged after her, Austin's tastebuds pinged with the flavor of tart cherries; his gustatory synesthesia was acting up, but not in a way he minded.

Of all the sensations his synesthesia brought—the flavors that sometimes accompanied feelings and emotions —tart cherry was probably his favorite. When he got this taste, it meant he'd received good news on a case he was working. In life, they were one of his favorite fruits, and cherry season in the Pacific Northwest was one of his favorite times of the year. Today the taste of tart cherries meant Austin and his team were finally onto something.

Samantha hadn't used some sophisticated algorithm or hacking software to figure out which of the three churches the call had come from. In fact, the technique had been something so easy even Austin could have done it. That is, *if* he'd thought of it.

Since they already had the audio of the call from the priest to the Island County Sheriff's Department, she had already done the work of isolating the background noise. There had been some unusual instrument playing, which sound analysis had determined to be a baroque organ. A quick YouTube search had allowed her to pull up videos of services and concerts from all three churches.

Only one of the three had a baroque organ, and that led them to Father Joseph Moretti of St. Gabriel the Archangel Church.

CHAPTER NINE

THE COOL, dim interior of St. Gabriel the Archangel Church was a stark contrast to the bright day outside. As Austin trailed Kendall inside, he saw that the church was modest but well-maintained, with polished wooden pews, stained glass windows depicting various saints, and a large organ at the back of the sanctuary. The scents of polished wood and incense hung in the air.

They found Father Joseph Moretti in the small office adjacent to the sanctuary. He was in his fifties, with salt-and-pepper hair and a kind, weathered face. He wore simple priestly attire—black pants, a white shirt, and a clerical collar. He looked up from a stack of paperwork and smiled warmly as they approached.

"Good afternoon, Father Moretti," Kendall said. "We're Detectives Shaw and Austin from the Kitsap County Sheriff's Department. We'd like to speak with you if you have a moment."

"A bit far from home," Father Moretti replied, setting his pen down and removing his glasses, which he left to hang around his neck just above his cross. "But of course."

Moretti's eyes were perceptive, though somewhat shifty, and Austin thought he saw an odd expression pass over his face. Not enough to raise suspicion, but something to be noted.

"I was just catching up on some paperwork," he said. "My doctor says it's good for me to move around at least once an hour. I don't like to stay idle and there's always work to be done around a church. You can follow me if you don't mind."

Austin and Kendall nodded, following the priest as he walked through the building.

"We just have a few questions," Kendall began.

The priest turned to look at her, smiled and nodded, but his facial expression made it clear he wasn't yet ready to engage them verbally. He beckoned them forward with a hand signal, then stalled briefly in a doorway that opened to the sanctuary. Inspecting the setup carefully, he said, "Have to make sure everything is set in place for the next service."

And, Austin thought, he wanted to ensure that no one was there to hear what they were going to talk about. Austin guessed that Moretti knew why they were there, and had mixed feelings about calling the police regarding something someone had said in confession.

Kendall shot Austin a frustrated look, but they continued following the priest in silence, taking in the serene environment of the church.

Father Moretti led Kendall and Austin to a storage room off the main hallway, where a large box labeled *DONATIONS* awaited attention. "See what I mean," he said, "always work to be done." He began organizing the contents, placing clothes, canned goods, and various household items on shelves. "Now, what questions do you have for me?" he asked, never breaking motion.

"Father Moretti," Kendall began, "we need to ask you

about the phone call regarding the deceased person found in the water beneath Deception Pass Bridge." Her speech was hurried, a sharp contrast to the quiet of the church and the priest's slow, decisive movements.

Father Moretti paused, glancing at Austin with a serious expression. "I understand your position, detectives, but the information was given to me under the sacrament of confession."

"So you knew that was why we're here?" Austin asked.

He sighed. "Honestly, I expected it, though I thought it would be our local people. Perhaps I even *wanted* someone to find out it was me who made the call."

"Father, we think it was murder." Kendall was trying to garner the priest's attention, but Austin thought Father Moretti might not be comfortable interacting with Kendall. Perhaps because she was female, or perhaps because her aggressive tone didn't fit well in the church.

"You must know that, as a priest, I am bound by the seal of confession, which means I cannot divulge anything said to me in that context, not even to the authorities."

"And yet," Kendall said, "you did exactly that."

"I never gave a name."

"Think God would buy that?" Kendall replied.

Moretti grimaced, but didn't reply. He slid forward four large cans of corn from the back of the shelf and placed an identical can of corn behind them. Austin had once ordered a number ten can of the same brand for his café, and he and his customers hadn't cared for it any more than the donating parishioners for this church had. He hoped the church had enough strong spices to mask the unpalatable elements.

Austin tilted his head slightly to meet Moretti's eyes. "I appreciate that you're making a distinction between alerting the police to a body and giving us the name of the person who told you about it, Father, but any information you could provide would help us."

"And it would also clear you as a suspect," Kendall added.

Austin shot her a look. Moretti wasn't a suspect—at least not as far as Austin was concerned—and he didn't look happy about the threat.

Moretti continued sorting through the donations, shaking his head. "I know what you are doing, Detective Shaw. But the sanctity of confession is absolute. It's one of the most sacred tenets of my faith. Even if it means obstructing an investigation, I cannot and will not break that ecclesiastical vow."

Austin frowned, but nodded his head in understanding.

"You must understand how frustrating this is for us." Kendall was growing more impatient. "Someone out there knows something about this death, and we've found that it's connected to two others, at least."

"I do understand, truly," Moretti said gently. "And I can't tell you how sorry I am to hear that it may be part of a pattern. But my duty to God and the church must come first. This confidentiality protects the trust between a priest and the confessor. Without that..." he trailed off, shaking his head.

Austin came in with a more gentle tone. "Is there anything at all you can tell us that might help, without breaking your vow?"

Father Moretti sighed deeply. "I wish there were."

Austin leaned in, trying one last time. "Can you at least tell us whether the diver who told you about the location of the body knew the deceased well? Part of the reason we want to speak with him is that we still don't know the man's identity, and we would like to reach out to friends or relatives if we can."

"I did not say it was a man, and how did you know it was a diver?" Moretti hesitated, looking at the ground.

Austin and Kendall exchanged glances, noting the inadvertent revelation. It was a small lead, but it was something.

"We didn't know for sure until just now," Kendall said, turning to Austin. "So we're looking for a female diver who's advanced enough to dive under the bridge and did so in the last week or so. Can't be too long of a list."

Moretti's eyes widened, and he quickly tried to recover. "I misspoke. I... I cannot say more. Please understand, I have a deeply devout relationship with God and a sacred responsibility to my congregants."

Kendall took the lull in the conversation as a chance to lighten the mood. "Looks like you are preparing for a charity event or something?"

"We host the largest fundraiser for the homeless and poor in the county each summer," Moretti explained. "Donations pour in from all over. Books from local authors, gift cards to local restaurants and spas. All sorts of stuff. Some things will just go to our pantry to feed the needy."

Austin perused the various items on one of the non-food shelves—a gift card to a local Italian restaurant, a piece of paper that described a three-day getaway at a local cabin that was used as an Airbnb, valued at over $1,000. Then Austin saw a name he recognized plastered across the front cover of a book. David Dierdrick Zwart was a neighbor in Hansville who'd risen to prominence recently for a series of mystery novels that featured local settings. Austin saw him in the café from time to time and the guy had always struck him as aloof, possibly downright pompous.

But it was the last piece of paper for the auction that truly grabbed his attention. It offered six scuba lessons from a local diving company, *Dive or Die*. The logo was a line drawing of a woman wearing diving gear in a Rosie the

Riveter pose making the "everything's okay" hand signal with the fingers of her flexed arm.

Austin touched Kendall on her shoulder. "Ready to head out?" he asked.

The look he gave her left no room for anything other than an answer in the affirmative.

Outside, Austin explained the donation form with the name of the dive shop. "How likely is it that there is more than one member of this church who owns a dive shop?"

"Not very," Kendall said.

Austin was already pulling up the name of the business on his phone. But it turned out, they didn't even need that. A group of women were walking into the church carrying boxes and chatting excitedly. More donations for the auction, Austin assumed.

Kendall was on it. "Excuse me," she said, walking up to them. "We're looking for a woman. I can't remember her name, but we met her in a class through *Dive or Die* and someone said if she isn't in her scuba gear, we might find her here."

"Oh, you must mean Carla Rivera," one of the women said pleasantly.

"Yes, that's right, Carla. Have you seen her?"

"I'm sure she's swimming about somewhere. You're not going to catch me in the water, but you rarely catch her out of it."

"Except on Sundays, of course," one of the other women corrected.

"Oh, yes," the first woman said. "I don't think she's missed a single Sunday service."

CHAPTER TEN

THE DIVE SHOP was located at the end of a little street off the main strip of downtown Oak Harbor, just a few blocks from the church and about fifteen minutes from the Deception Pass Bridge.

Pausing about ten feet from the glass door marked with the same logo they'd seen at the church, Kendall touched Austin's arm. "I think it's pretty safe to say that just by our natures, I should be the bad cop and you should be the good cop."

"I don't really follow those clichés," Austin said, "although I do understand their utility in some situations. And I guess it worked with Father Moretti."

"Nice job on that misdirection, by the way," Kendall said. "Calling the parishioner a *male* diver."

"Figured it must be a serious diver, so why not see if I could trip him up. But it was the donation form that broke this thing open."

Kendall frowned. "I've got fifty bucks that says this woman is actually our killer. I'm planning to push a little bit and see what she gives up. You, you're a little more affable by nature. Plus, you're a good-looking guy. If she likes men, she'll be predisposed to liking you. And if she likes you, she'll be predisposed to *dislike* me."

"Why's that?" Austin asked.

"Because I look like I do," Kendall said. She was half-joking, but Kendall *did* enjoy pointing out how good looking she was.

"Women aren't really like that, are they?" Austin asked.

"Oh, it's definitely a thing," Kendall said. "At least among some women."

Austin shrugged. "What makes you think she's the killer?"

"You know as well as I do, killers like to revisit the scene of the crime. My guess, Carla Rivera was revisiting where she dumped the body for kicks, then told Moretti about it because she realized she couldn't live without someone talking about her work in the papers. Or maybe she didn't even go back to the scene. She could have dumped the body there a week or two ago, then told Moretti, now that I think about it."

"But it's usually *serial* killers who like to revisit their crimes. This doesn't strike me as that."

Kendall raised a perfectly groomed eyebrow. "Even though we have multiple deaths that are all very similar?"

It wasn't a bad point, but something in this case didn't feel like a serial killer to Austin. He couldn't explain it.

Kendall pushed open the glass door, which triggered a little bell, alerting the staff to their arrival. A bulletin board near the entrance held a collage of snapshots—smiling faces of divers, some mid-dive, others posing and pointing at the sea creatures they happened upon during their dives.

Wandering into the small shop, Austin was immediately enveloped by the scent of seawater and neoprene. The wooden floorboards creaked gently underfoot, giving audible protest to the years of wear from salt-crusted boots and fins. The walls were lined with shelves, each meticulously organized yet bearing the evidence of frequent use in chipped paint and streaked markings left from shuffling around the diving masks, snorkels, and fins, which sat lining the shelves in various colors and sizes.

There was one staff member present, a woman whom Austin assumed was Carla. She was average height and clearly strong from hour after hour in the water. "Are you Carla Rivera?" he asked, his tone professional but also warm and polite.

The woman smiled, but looked at Austin questioningly. "Have we met?"

Austin noticed she didn't answer the question.

The counter she stood behind was adorned with a scattering of dive accessories: waterproof dive slates, compasses, and dive knives encased in sheaths. Behind the counter, a pegboard displayed a selection of scuba tanks, their metallic bodies glinting under the soft overhead lights. The tanks were neatly arranged by size and capacity, from compact pony bottles to larger aluminum tanks for deeper dives.

Kendall let out her bad cop vibes with, "Ms. Rivera, I'm Detective Kendall Shaw and this is Detective Austin. We're from the Kitsap County police, and we want to talk to you about the body you found, or *claim* you found, under the bridge."

The woman made the sign of the cross and started whispering something to herself, a quiet prayer.

Just then a black cat leapt up from behind the counter and hissed at them. Austin lurched back instinctively, but Kendall smiled. She looked from Carla to the cat, the cat to Carla.

"You think you can intimidate us with a black cat?" she asked.

Carla reached out and pet the animal. "This is Midnight. And no, I'm not trying to intimidate you. She just isn't especially friendly. You might know the type."

Kendall looked over at Austin and threw him an *I told you so* look. "She looks like something that just crawled out of Stephen King's *Pet Sematary*," Kendall said.

Midnight paced back and forth along the counter, keeping her eyes on Kendall the whole time.

"We don't have a lot of time," Kendall continued, "and I suggest you don't bother beating around the bush or lying. Are you the woman who found the body under Deception Pass Bridge a few days ago?"

"Who told you I was?" Carla asked.

Kendall placed both hands on the driftwood log counter and leaned in. She had a few inches on Carla, and Austin could tell Carla was flustered, even intimidated. But, for a long time, Kendall didn't say anything. Austin was fine to go along with the act.

Finally, Kendall said, "Seeing as *we're* the police, we'll be the ones asking the questions here, okay?"

Carla nodded, then murmured, "Yes, I was the woman. I told Father Moretti in confidence."

"He wasn't the one who told us you were the witness," Austin pointed out. "He didn't break your confidence."

Carla was going to say something, but Kendall held up a hand in Austin's direction. "Witness? Or *suspect*?"

"No, no, no," Carla stammered. "We were just on a dive, and I found the body."

"*We?*" Kendall asked.

Midnight hissed again, and Austin took a slight step back. As much as he loved dogs, he wasn't so sure about cats.

He had never had one because Fiona was allergic and their personalities had just never made sense to him. One thing he was sure of was that Midnight did *not* like Kendall. At all.

"It was a date," Carla said, looking down at the counter.

"A date with who?" Kendall demanded.

"Some jerk named Ben."

"Please tell us about it from the beginning," Austin said.

Over the next five minutes, Carla walked them through the morning she'd found the body. After meeting Ben at the site, she'd provided gear and, when they were situated, she'd led them into the water. "Everything went fine at first," she said. "I mean, he complained about the gear a little, but it was all top notch. He didn't know what he was talking about."

She spent the next few minutes describing all of the amazing creatures she saw during the dive, then concluded with, "Ben disappeared, I saw the body, then I went back up to the surface and found him texting on his phone."

"Okay if I ask you something?" Austin had turned up the warmth dial in his voice as much as he could muster.

Carla nodded.

"This guy, Ben—are you afraid of him?"

Carla looked up at the ceiling as though contemplating this for the first time. "Afraid? No, but I do hate the guy." She made the sign of the cross. "I shouldn't say *hate*. I do not like him, okay? Playing in the water requires humility. Tell you one thing, you'll never see me on a dive with that guy ever again. He was arrogant and reckless."

"Was?" Kendall asked. "Did you kill him like you killed the old man?"

The look on Carla's face was somewhere between shock and anger. "I've never killed anyone," she said. "I meant 'was' because I told him I'd never see him again after that disastrous date. He's a *was* to me."

"Can you prove that?" Kendall asked.

Carla turned and began rummaging through the items on a messy table behind the counter, finally pulling her phone from under a stack of papers. She opened a text thread and handed the phone to Kendall.

Austin watched over her shoulder as Kendall scrolled through the messages. He couldn't read as fast as Kendall, but when she'd finished, Kendall handed the phone back to Carla. "Assuming that's real, it appears to be a normal text thread, ending with you telling Ben you don't want to see him again. In the thread, you mentioned a video camera. An underwater camera. Do you record your dives?"

Carla reached out and took Midnight in her arms, stroking her. This was to soothe Carla more than the cat, Austin thought.

"I always record my dives, but I don't want to talk about that." Carla looked up at the ceiling again and appeared to be holding back tears. "It was just awful to bump into that dead man. The water is sacred to me and I... how could someone..."

"I'm not sure you get the picture here," Kendall said, her voice tight and demanding. "It's not about what *you* want to talk about. It's about—"

Austin interjected, cutting Kendall off, his voice low. "Carla, this is very serious. If you have a video of a crime scene and don't share it with the police..." He shook his head.

Carla set the cat down on the counter and then, as though making a decision, turned and walked to the back office.

"Come with me," she said.

CHAPTER ELEVEN

IT TOOK LONGER than Austin wanted, but eventually Carla was able to transfer the video from her dive camera to her computer and send a compressed file to Kendall's phone.

Kendall had wanted to watch it with Carla in the room, but Austin had convinced her to take it outside to the car. They could always watch it with her later if they had questions, but Austin believed Carla was genuinely traumatized by the events, and there was no need to put her through it again by forcing her to watch the video.

Huddled next to each other in the front seats of the car, they stared down at Kendall's phone. Carla had explained that it was an underwater head-mounted camera, so what they were watching was essentially what she had seen on the dive.

She'd started taking videos of all her dives because a business partner had encouraged her to start doing more social media marketing. She'd rarely watched a whole video, instead just finding the best-looking clips and posting them on Instagram and Facebook as advertisements for her dive shop. Austin himself had never been on a dive, so he found the whole thing fascinating.

The footage provided a clear view of the underwater scene from Carla's point of view as she navigated beneath the Deception Pass Bridge. The camera captured the murky, yet vibrant undersea world, starting with the rocky seabed covered in colorful anemones and schools of rockfish darting through the water. Lingcods blended into their surroundings, barely distinguishable from the rocks they lay against.

As she progressed, the focus shifted to various marine life encounters, including a curious interaction with a giant Pacific octopus gently probing its surroundings with a tentacle. The camera panned up to reveal swaying kelp forests, filtering sunlight into a display of underwater luminescence.

The tranquility of the dive was momentarily disrupted when the camera suddenly focused on a rocky outcrop. Something had clearly caught Carla's attention—a shape obscured by the swaying kelp and shifting shadows, difficult to make out at first. The camera moved closer, revealing a human-like form lying against the rocks. Carla paused, hovering near the figure, which appeared disturbingly still. Details were hard to discern as fish swam around and over the form, which seemed eerily out of place in the vibrant activity of sea life.

But Austin had no doubt it was their John Doe.

Reacting to the sight, the camera movements became hurried and less steady as Carla made a rapid ascent towards the surface. Austin observed what appeared to be increasing agitation in her pace, signaled by the faster passing of the sea flora and the bubbling trail left by the ascent.

"Go back for a moment," Austin said. "To where she approaches the body. I think I saw something." Kendall did, and Austin saw again what he thought he'd seen before. "Pause it right there." He touched the screen. "Is he wearing a shoe?"

"It sure looks like a shoe," Kendall agreed.

"Keep it rolling," Austin said.

They watched as Carla swam away. As she ascended, she turned back to look again at the body. Light was streaming through the water and illuminated both the body and the rock formation below it.

"Pause it now," Austin said. "Look there. No shoe. Where'd it go?"

"She bumped it, maybe."

The deceased had been found without shoes, so this was clearly something that had been missed in the initial dive.

Kendall turned to him, eyebrows raised. "I'm going back in to rent some dive equipment."

Austin frowned. He was already pulling out his phone. "No. We're leaving this to the pros. I've got the dive team on speed dial. Didn't you see that poster in the dive shop warning you not to get caught in a whirlpool or strong current? I'm not willing to sit on the shore and watch you try not to drown in that strait where I can't do anything to save you. Not today."

The poster's headline had been in large capital lettering with a bold red font that read: *DECEPTION PASS=A DECEPTIVE CURRENT.*

As the sun began to set, Austin watched as the two-woman dive crew disappeared below the surface.

It had taken three hours for the crew to arrive. The

coming darkness would make the task of finding the stray shoe more difficult, but the divers had headlamps on their helmets that assured Austin that, if a shoe or any other evidence was down there, they would find it.

They still didn't know the identity of their John Doe, and the knowledge ate away at Austin. He only hoped that the shoe, if found, might provide some clue. This case was different than others he'd worked.

To Austin, anyone who served in the Seabees in World War Two was a hero, and yet this man had become one of the forgotten. A man with no friends. A man without money. A man without status. A man with no family, or at least no family close enough to notice—or, worse yet—to *care* that he was gone.

About fifteen minutes after they had disappeared into the water, Austin saw a pale light start to rise from the depths. A head emerged, then another.

Austin walked a couple yards down toward the bank of the water. Kendall, who had been on her phone, followed him.

The diver was breathing heavily and holding up a single shoe. "Just found the one," she said. "And nothing else."

Austin thanked her and pulled a small flashlight off his belt to examine the shoe. It was a size nine leather loafer, one that looked like it had cost a pretty penny, and not just from a few days in the water. Maybe this guy had money after all.

"Well, look at that," Austin said as he noticed the writing in thick black marker on the inside heel of the shoe.

A name.

He held it up to Kendall.

"Whoa," Kendall said. "Who writes their name on the inside of their shoes?"

"Kids at camp," Austin said. "People with dementia and

those who care for them. And, occasionally, people who live in tight quarters and have similar shoes." He read the name again. "I guess our Seabee went by the name of Jack Ulner."

CHAPTER TWELVE

THE MAN CARLA had gone diving with was named Ben Davis and, from what she'd said, he liked to hang out at a downtown Mediterranean restaurant most evenings. So that's where they were headed.

"Even though Carla made him out to be a regular jerk," Kendall said as Austin flicked on the headlights and pulled into traffic, "it's quite possible he's something worse than that."

"A killer?" Austin asked.

"Or just an abuser. Who knows with people these days?"

Carla had told them that diving under the Deception Pass Bridge that day had been Ben's idea. Although Carla had assured them that the tides were safe enough to make the dive, they were far from ideal conditions and, initially, she'd argued to wait for a longer slack tide to be predicted. But Ben had been insistent that they dive there that day.

"Just thinking," Kendall continued, "maybe he wanted to revisit the scene of his crime or, perhaps, he wanted to lead Carla to discover the body—maybe he saw it as some kind of sick and twisted way to impress her."

"Bit of a stretch," Austin said, "but it wouldn't be the strangest thing I'd seen happen on a date."

In his experience, some killers start off *thinking* they want to hide the body and get away scot-free. But then, when they don't see news of their evil pop up in newspapers in the following days, they actually work against themselves, hoping for the body to get discovered. It was an odd kind of narcissism that wasn't common, but also wasn't unheard of.

In any case, they wanted to get Ben's side of the story and ask whether he'd seen anything that hadn't been captured on the video. If the dive had ended the way Carla had explained it, it was possible Ben had seen something and didn't say anything since their date came to a rocky end right after they surfaced.

Austin slowed and took a soft right turn, heading for the center of downtown.

"We really need to get our pups together," Kendall said.

Austin gave her a strange look. She had a way of bringing up topics that were not at all in line with where his mind was.

"That would be great," Austin said, a bit flummoxed.

In the fall of last year, Austin had been in Brooklyn and Manhattan for a while working on the case of his deceased wife. Kendall had really stepped up for him, staying in his apartment for a while and taking care of Run. She'd even seen Run through a difficult health situation, which, thankfully, was now completely resolved. Run had many good years in front of her.

"Let's get them together for a beach play date," Kendall said.

"Absolutely," Austin replied. "You sent the name back to Samantha?"

"I did," Kendall said. "If that man exists in any database

anywhere, we will know fairly soon. I'm actually surprised we haven't heard anything already."

Austin turned onto the main street. "What was the name of the place?"

"Mediterranean restaurant." She pointed across the street to the left. "There. Kebab Palace. Park anywhere. Oh wait, don't park. Hold on. Just slow down."

"What is it?" Austin asked.

"Quiet," Kendall said.

Austin slowed, glancing in the direction of the restaurant. It appeared to be an informal place, with plastic tables and chairs and a white linoleum floor. A fluorescent light flickered, and the "P" in the sign out front was half burned out.

"Did you ever work narcotics?" Kendall asked.

Austin shook his head. "Not directly, but a lot of the cases I've been involved in—"

Kendall held up a finger, silencing him. They waited and then, after a couple minutes, she pointed. "See the guy in the black hat?"

Austin looked across the street to where a man in his late forties or early fifties was walking up to a car and handing something through the window. The man in the passenger seat of the vehicle seemed to reach out to shake his hand.

"That's the second one in the last three minutes," Kendall said.

Austin stopped the car, partially blocking traffic. Kendall held up her phone, showing Austin a picture of Ben Davis, which Carla had texted her.

"That's him," Austin said. "She didn't mention that he was a drug dealer. Why do you think she would leave that out?"

Kendall shrugged. "Maybe she didn't know. I once dated

a guy for three weeks before finding out he'd done three years for distribution of LSD."

"How'd that work out?" Austin asked dryly.

"It didn't."

Davis now had his hands in his pockets and was strolling down the street. They watched as he got into a small gray minivan, an older model with the bumper duct taped into place. He started the car and pulled down the street.

Austin made a casual U-turn and followed. After a few blocks, the van turned right down what appeared to be a residential street. Austin followed a good hundred yards behind. He was fairly practiced at driving so as not to alert the person he was tailing.

The van turned again, and Kendall, who had been reading on her phone, said suddenly, "Well, it turns out Jack Ulner is definitely not our John Doe, despite what was on the inside of his shoe."

"How's that?" Austin asked. "I mean, how can you be so sure?"

"Because, according to Samantha, Jack Ulner is still alive."

Austin grimaced. "Uh, that doesn't make any sense."

"I know it doesn't. We either have a guy by the same name or, we have a guy who took off with Jack Ulner's shoes."

"I'm guessing it's the latter. Are they sure they have the same shoe we saw in the diving video and the owner of it is definitely alive?"

"They say they're certain it's the shoe. And Jack Ulner filed taxes only a month ago."

Austin ran his hand through his hair. "There's our proof of life then."

"Our still alive Jack Ulner lives in a residential commu-nity only fifteen minutes from our office. Big Valley Road in

Poulsbo. Samantha didn't call the facility because she didn't want to alert them to the investigation. She is waiting to hear from us what our next move will be."

Austin shook his head. "Wow."

The van pulled up to a small one-story house and Ben Davis got out and began walking toward the front door.

Austin, who'd been distracted with the news of Jack Ulner being alive, had gotten a little bit too close and he'd had to slow suddenly when Davis pulled into his driveway.

Davis strolled up to his front door, then stopped and turned before opening it. He squinted toward their car, then suddenly took off in a full sprint, disappearing between his and a neighbor's house.

PART 2

CLEAR AS MUD

CHAPTER THIRTEEN

"I'M GOING AFTER HIM," Kendall said, swinging her door open before Austin had even fully stopped the car.

"Wait," Austin said, but it was too late.

Kendall had already leapt the curb and sprinted through the gap between the houses, following Davis.

Quickly, Austin called Sheriff Derby, letting him know that Kendall was pursuing Davis toward the downtown and asking for backup. After being assured that they'd have multiple officers intercept them, Austin decided there was no chance for him to catch up, so he may as well inspect the property.

The sun had set completely now and the little front yard that appeared to belong to Davis was lit only by a motion-sensor light that had flipped on when their suspect walked up to the porch. A concrete walkway led to three steps up to the tiny cement porch and a white front door.

Next to Davis's gray van in the driveway was a 1970s Chevy, set up on blocks as though someone had started to fix it months or possibly years ago, then left it there to rust. There was a thick layer of dust covering the thing and one of the rear windows was missing. But it wasn't the car that held Austin's attention.

It was the gravel underneath it.

Kendall sprinted through the narrow space between the houses, dodging trash cans and recycling bins, her heart pounding in her chest. She could hear her own breath, quick and sharp, as she pushed herself to move faster. The streetlamps cast long shadows that made it difficult to see clearly. For a moment, she thought she had lost him and she slowed, scanning a back yard and listening intently.

Then she heard the faint snap of a branch to her left. Without hesitation, Kendall veered in that direction, leaping over a low chain link fence and then another. She landed with a soft thud on the other side, coming out onto another residential street. She looked both ways, her eyes darting across the landscape, and then she saw him.

Ben Davis was sprinting away, his silhouette just visible.

"Stop!" Kendall yelled, her voice cutting through the quiet evening. "Kitsap County Police!"

But Davis didn't stop. Pausing for only a moment to glance back, he stumbled, careened into a tree and fell. But just as quickly he was back on his feet and cutting around a corner.

Austin crouched, shining his flashlight at the driveway.

He wasn't certain, but the small gray and blue stones appeared to be a good match for those found in the pocket of the deceased veteran who'd been found under Deception Pass Bridge, as well as the other victims.

He'd need to take a sample back to the office to be sure, but this was certainly something pointing toward Davis's guilt. Pulling out his cell phone, he walked up the steps to the little cement porch as he dialed Lucy. As experienced as he was as a detective, it struck Austin that this was his first case as an actual member of law enforcement in years. Not only that, he wasn't certain about all the protocols in Washington state. As a private investigator, he'd felt a little more free to break them when necessary. Now, he had to think about a potential prosecution and answer to Lucy—who was on his side—and also to a local prosecutor, who might blame him for ruining a case if he didn't follow protocol.

Lucy picked up after five rings.

"It's Austin," he said. "You've probably heard from Samantha that we have a name. We thought it was the name of our John Doe, but, apparently, he is alive."

"I heard," Lucy said. "We are already looking into it."

"Kendall is pursuing someone on foot. Heading back toward the commercial district. I called for—"

"Alone?" she asked. "Where are you? Wait, hold on."

From the porch, Austin peered into the kitchen through a small window. It was mostly blocked by blinds, but a single missing slat offered Austin a partial view.

The kitchen was modest and unremarkable, with plain white cabinets and slightly worn countertops. The appliances were a mismatched assortment, a white refrigerator with a few magnets and notes stuck to it, an older gas stove, and a microwave that looked like it had warmed a hundred bowls of soup since the last time it had been cleaned. The linoleum floor had a few scuff marks, and the table in the center of the room was cluttered with mail, a couple empty coffee mugs, and a newspaper.

As Austin scanned the room, something in the far corner caught his eye. There were several wire racks stacked on a small table, each filled with mushrooms in various stages of drying. Two small fans were set up to aid the drying process, and brown paper bags full of freshly picked mushrooms were scattered around. At first glance, it seemed like a typical setup for drying foraged mushrooms, something not uncommon in the area. But then Austin noticed something unusual.

"Okay, I'm back," Lucy said.

"Wait a sec," Austin said, letting his arm and phone drop to his side and manually narrowing the beam of his flashlight.

Among the drying mushrooms were some that had distinctive blue bruising on their stems and caps, a telltale sign of psychedelic varieties. He also saw a few glass jars labeled with scientific names that he didn't recognize offhand, along with a digital scale and some drying agents.

While foraging and drying mushrooms was fairly common in the area, this setup suggested something more than a hobby. It wasn't hard to put two and two together. Ben Davis was involved in harvesting psychedelic mushrooms and was selling them out of a Kebab shop in Oak Harbor.

Austin brought the phone up to his ear.

Lucy was practically yelling into the phone. "Austin, are you there?"

"Sorry. I... Kendall took off before I could stop her. Derby is sending officers to assist. I'm at the front door of the man who we believe could be involved, and there's gravel that matches. Is that enough for me to enter his home without a warrant? Probable cause?"

"No, that's probably not enough," Lucy said, her voice firm.

"What if I see evidence of a drug crime from outside

the house?" Austin asked, his eyes still fixed on the mushrooms.

"Then, well, it kinda depends."

"On what?"

"On how sure you are that you're right."

Kendall was in better shape and younger than Davis, and she could feel herself gaining on him with every stride. They weaved through the residential neighborhood, darting past parked cars, leaping over garden beds, and squeezing through narrow gaps between houses. Kendall's focus was razor-sharp, her senses heightened by the chase.

Davis noticed the flashing blue and white lights coming around a corner and tried to lose them, making a sudden turn and dashing into a large backyard. He hurdled a child's bicycle lying on its side and nearly stumbled, but kept his footing and continued on as the lights faded from view.

Kendall followed with ease, her training and fitness giving her the edge.

As they neared the end of a block, Kendall realized he was slowing. With one final burst of speed, she closed the gap and lunged forward, her hands outstretched, and tackled him from behind.

They both went down hard, rolling across the ground. Kendall scrambled to pin him down, using her weight to keep him immobile.

"You're not going anywhere Ben," she said, her voice hard. But before she could reach her cuffs he brought up a knee, connecting with her thigh and knocking her to the side.

CHAPTER FOURTEEN

THE FRONT DOOR wasn't even locked.

Austin had knocked multiple times, then cracked it and called in a warning. The place was silent, and Carla had mentioned that she didn't think Ben lived with anyone. In fact, her exact quote had been, "I thought he was homeless."

Stepping inside, he called one more time, "Kitsap County Sheriff's Department! Is anyone home?"

Austin moved cautiously, his eyes scanning for any signs of movement. He could see why it would benefit Ben to have the women he was dating believe he was homeless before admitting to living here. The living room was cluttered with old furniture and piles of magazines and newspapers. Dust covered every surface, and a musty smell lingered in the air, and it wasn't just from the mushrooms.

Altogether, the house was only about eight hundred square feet. It had two small bedrooms, a filthy bathroom, a living room, and the disheveled kitchen that, apparently, was used only for re-heating food and drying mushrooms. The mushroom racks dominated one corner, covered with hundreds of bluish capped mushrooms with long, thin stems. Small fans hummed quietly, keeping the air circulating, and the digital scale and glass jars completed the scene. There was no doubt he was dealing.

On the table Austin found a stack of business cards and had to read the words twice before believing he hadn't gotten second-hand high from mushroom fumes. He'd seen a lot during his tenure as a detective in New York City. More murders than he wanted to think about, drug crimes of all sorts, even some of the most twisted serial killers the world had ever seen.

But the brand advertised on the business card stopped him in his tracks.

Ben Davis: Psychedelics for Seniors.

Austin's mind raced. He thought back to the people in the front seat of the car whom he and Kendall had watched accept what Austin now assumed were psychedelic mushrooms from Ben Davis. They had definitely been on the older side—sixty at least, now that Austin thought about it.

Standing there in the kitchen, he put the whole thing together in his head. Marijuana had been made legal in Washington state years ago, and psychedelic mushrooms, while not legal, had been partially decriminalized. It was possible that Ben Davis was foraging them himself and selling them specifically to seniors. It wasn't a stretch to imagine that someone, or multiple people, had threatened to turn him in and he'd killed them. Or, possibly, that a few of his customers had had adverse reactions to the drugs—deadly ones—and that Davis had needed to dispose of the bodies to protect his business, and his freedom.

Austin snapped a few photographs with his phone and then walked back out to the porch, dialing Lucy. When she picked up, he said, "I need an evidence van. I need to know precisely how to handle this. But I think we may have found our guy."

Kendall leapt forward, tackling Ben from behind as he tried to stand. They both went down hard, rolling across the ground. Ben resisted, flailing and trying to push her off, but his superior strength was no match for Kendall's skill and training. Or her endurance.

He was doughy and not in good shape, already out of breath and wheezing.

Taking him by the wrist, Kendall twisted his arm behind his back, then pressed her knee into it.

"Stay down," she commanded. She patted him down quickly, finding no weapons. After a few seconds, Ben stopped resisting, clearly realizing he was outmatched.

She cuffed him and stood him up, keeping a firm grip on his arm. "You're under arrest," she said, her eyes meeting his.

His shoulders sagged in defeat, and he was still struggling to catch his breath as Kendall led him back toward his house.

"That bitch!" Davis exclaimed suddenly. His voice was higher than she'd expected, and whinier. The kind of voice that puts you off immediately, no matter what the words are.

"Are you speaking about Carla?" Kendall asked.

"Yeah, and I was hoping never to see her again, or hear her name again. Did she send you after me because I ditched her on the dive?" He didn't wait for a reply, just continued on. "She gave me crappy equipment, she's an illegal immigrant, and her business is shady as hell. You should be looking into her, not me. How did she even know what I do for a living, anyway? Why are you even here? Why did you follow me?"

Kendall didn't need to answer, and she wasn't going to. It didn't happen much outside of television shows, but sometimes a suspect would just talk and talk and give themselves up in a million ways before figuring out that they should shut up.

"You didn't see anything," Davis continued, "I didn't admit to anything. If this is about that body they found—yeah, I saw that in the papers—I had absolutely nothing to do with that. If you ask me, Carla probably took that guy diving and got him killed with crappy equipment! If I had stayed down there with her, you might have found me there as well."

By the time they got back to Davis's house, the man had finally stopped talking and Austin was sitting on the steps.

"Who's that jerk?" Davis asked, struggling against the cuffs and attempting to point at Austin.

"That's my partner, Detective Thomas Austin," Kendall replied.

She stopped, noticing the gravel under the car that was up on blocks. "Interesting," she said, pointing at it. "Where did you get that?"

"It was here when I got the house, you idiot," Davis said.

Kendall cocked her head and smiled at him. "You and I are going to have a great time together. You're going to grow to like me, trust me, depend on me."

"Lawyer," Davis said. "I'm not saying anything else until I talk with my lawyer."

"Who's your lawyer?" Kendall asked. "I'll call him myself."

"And if I don't have one?"

Even better, Kendall thought. But what she said was, "Of course, one will be provided to you."

CHAPTER FIFTEEN

Thursday

THE NEXT MORNING, Austin woke early.

Run had snuggled into bed with him in the middle of the night, which she usually didn't do. She was a dog who liked small amounts of affection, and usually on her own terms. When she *did* decide to sleep in his bed, which he was happy to allow, she usually took a position at the bottom, where she could avoid any unintended contact.

But this morning, out of nowhere, as he lay on his back staring up at the ceiling from his bed, she crawled onto his stomach and began licking his face. After a few minutes, Austin stood up and Run eyed him eagerly, then darted toward the door. Stopping and sitting abruptly, she looked back as though saying, "You're coming, right?" Then she offered up one of her polite indoor barks, a bark that said, *pay attention to me.*

"What is it?" he asked.

When he opened the bedroom door she beelined for

the kitchen. When he walked into the kitchen, she was eating from her food bowl as though she had been starving.

Then it hit him—he'd fed her dinner late the night before and hadn't stuck to their routine.

He usually fed her once a day at 5 or 6 PM, which is what the veterinarian had recommended. And he usually dolloped a tablespoon of cottage cheese on top before watching her eat then taking her outside for a last potty break.

But last night she'd followed him into the bedroom *before* eating, probably because he'd gotten home so late and forgotten her *topper*. He must have shut the bedroom door, so she couldn't get to the dinner she'd left uneaten.

A pang of guilt hit his chest. Even with his simple bachelor lifestyle, he hadn't been able to make sure the only being he was responsible for, besides himself, had eaten her dinner.

He got the cottage cheese from the refrigerator and scooped her topper on the dry food. Run dug in eagerly. Austin pulled the pot from the refrigerator and poured himself a cold cup of coffee. Sitting at the little table in his kitchen, he took a sip. He usually made fresh coffee or at least microwaved his leftovers, but his energy was low, his mind distracted.

After Ben Davis lawyered up, they had brought him back to Kitsap County, where he was being held to meet with his lawyer in the morning. They had also looked into Jack Ulner a bit more and planned to interview him at 9 AM sharp.

But the biggest distraction running through his mind was that, as he'd pulled into Hansville a little after 8 PM the previous night, Austin had gotten a call from his mother.

His dad had taken a nasty fall, slipping on clothes he'd left on the floor. Apparently, he'd put on three shirts before dinner and had thrown the rest of the clothes from two of his dresser drawers around the room. He hadn't hit his head, thankfully, but he'd sprained both of his wrists and took a pretty good gash from sliding against the bedframe. His arm had needed six stitches.

It was protocol for the facility to call family right away and, when they did, his mother had taken herself to the emergency room, where she'd stayed with him through the rest of the evening while they got him stitched and bandaged. His mom, always a trooper, had sounded exhausted, and this had hit Austin hard. The inevitability of aging and becoming more frail, and having to count on others for basic needs, shook him to the core.

Even though he was sad about his dad, at least he had his mom. In the gray light of dawn, Austin looked around his cold, stark kitchen. Despite Run's warmth as she devoured her food, Austin was acutely aware that he was alone.

Forty-five minutes later, Austin sat in the back of the little community church in Hansville, where Pastor Johnson let him come early in the morning. Austin had sometimes gone to church with his parents as a child, but had lost touch with it as an adult.

And even though Pastor Johnson always encouraged him to come to a regular service, it never felt right to Austin. He had begun coming to this church because something in it triggered his synesthesia. Something in the smell reminded him of Fiona and comforted him. After solving her murder, he hadn't felt like he needed it in the same way, but there was something in it he needed this morning.

Despite his efforts to focus on the case, memories kept

passing through his mind, and it seemed as though there was nothing he could do to stop them. Since his mom had been in the Navy, he'd moved around a lot as a child. San Diego, Connecticut, even a short stint in Bremerton, Washington, not far from where he now lived.

Each time they would land in a new town, he and his dad would go to a grocery store for cheese and crackers. Then they would go to a gas station and buy some beef jerky or some candy. Then, they would always find a nearby beach.

Austin closed his eyes as the light began to seep through the windows of the church.

"Okay, it's time to bury my feet," his dad would say when they hit the beach.

Each time, Austin would bury his dad's feet in the sand, believing he could pile enough sand to make it so that his dad wouldn't be able to move. Austin always laughed when his father would say, "*Help! I can't move my feet, I can't move my feet.*"

And then Austin would dig in the sand, shoving it away like a dog working to bury a bone until his father jumped up and praised him for saving him from the incoming tide.

It wasn't until their third or fourth move that Austin realized his father had been tricking him. There was no amount of sand he could pile that would make it so his father couldn't simply lift his feet up. He must have been around seven years old when he realized that his dad had just been trying to entertain him.

In general, his dad didn't *play* with him. He wasn't an especially gregarious guy. So this was an especially fond memory.

Austin's father came from a time when dads didn't show as much affection as they seemed to show these days. That was okay, but somehow it made Austin both grateful and sad that his dad had pretended to be stuck in the sand. In retrospect, he could see that those little trips were his father's way of getting to know the new town, and a way for his father to support his mother to have time alone in the new house so she could unpack and organize things. When you move, not only do you have to figure out your routines in a new house, you also have to know where the grocery store, the gas station, and the beach are, after all.

Austin opened his eyes. It must have been around 7 AM as the light was now bright in the little church. Austin heard Pastor Johnson come in through the back door, probably getting ready to prepare meals for his biweekly food service for the homeless.

They usually shared nice little chats on the mornings when Austin found his way in here. This morning, Austin didn't feel like it.

Quietly, he stood and slipped out the front door.

CHAPTER SIXTEEN

AN HOUR LATER, Austin was standing at the whiteboard in the office, watched by Kendall, Lucy, Jimmy, and Samantha.

Lucy said, "I've got a conference call in ten minutes, Austin. You're going to have to keep the ball rolling on this. You and Kendall, that is. I need to make a report, though, so give me everything we've got. The condensed version." She sipped a cup of coffee, not nervously, but in a hurry, taking frequent drags from the cup like someone smoking a cigarette on an unsanctioned smoke break.

Lucy was on the young side to have been made lead detective and, though she was doing a great job, Austin thought sometimes she appeared to be in over her head. Not as an investigator, but when it came to politics.

"We've got three threads," Austin said, tapping the whiteboard with a pen. "Ben Davis runs a small, illegal business called *Psychedelics for Seniors*. Has similar gravel in his driveway to that found on the victims. We saw him dealing; we have the mushrooms, which we've confirmed with the lab are a few different forms of psychedelics. This is not a

Pablo Escobar thing from what we can tell. He strikes me as a guy who grew up as a rich kid and never wanted a real job, so he pieces a life together through family money and illicit mushrooms."

"He's a jackass," Kendall interrupted, "and a loser. And his voice is as grating as fingernails on a chalkboard."

Austin nodded, conceding the point. "My point is, he's not some major drug player. From what we can tell, he gathers psychedelic mushrooms in the forests..."

"And from cow pies, I'm sure," Kendall interrupted.

"He sells them to seniors," Austin continued, "advertising that they help with sciatic pain and anxiety and nerve issues. He will be meeting his lawyer this morning and—"

"Gretchen Vale," Lucy said, her voice full of disdain.

Austin's face must have shown how puzzled he was.

"Best defense attorney in the county," Jimmy said. "Or, worst, depending on your point of view."

"She's the best if you're a defendant," Lucy said. "Worst if you're us. And she's also best friends with County Commissioner Larsen."

Jimmy nodded. "Point is, we're not gonna get anything out of Ben Davis unless it's exactly what Gretchen Vale wants us to get."

Lucy sighed, rubbing her temples in a way that reminded Austin of Ridley.

"As we spoke about," Austin continued, "Davis was on the dive where the body was discovered. And I'd love to hear Counselor Vale's explanation for that."

"And we still don't have a name for our John Doe?" Lucy asked.

Austin shook his head. "Correct, there's only one Jack Ulner locally, and he's alive. Which leads us to the second thread. The deceased, John Doe, was wearing his shoes.

Ulner lives at a small assisted living facility in Poulsbo. We will be heading there directly after this meeting."

"So what we are thinking," Kendall said, "is that it's possible both the unnamed victim and the initial victims at Manette Bridge and Deception Pass were clients of Ben Davis. Perhaps they threatened to squeal on him, or perhaps they had an adverse reaction to his drugs and he killed them. Perhaps one of them overdosed or took their own life. We don't know yet, but we have some theories."

Lucy nodded.

Jimmy drummed his fingers on the table and turned to Samantha. "You're already looking into the gravel, right?"

"Visual inspection alone wasn't enough," Samantha said. "It looks similar, but we're running it by some experts and should have an answer soon. Plus, we're waiting on a report from a company that sells that type in Kitsap and Island counties. They're gonna give us a list of places that might have made orders in the last few years."

"Let's just hope it's not too long," Jimmy said.

Austin continued, "What I don't get is why Ben Davis would insist that he and Carla dive at a spot where he knew one of his victims to be."

"Because he's a sick bastard," Kendall said.

He'd known Kendall wasn't going to let this one go. On the drive back from Whidbey Island, she'd made it clear that she now believed Davis to be their killer, not Carla. Austin wondered whether she'd taken their tussle a little too personally, but he waved her on to make her case.

"Davis is the kind of guy," she began, "who convinces his date—whom he probably sought out because she was known to be a top diver—convinces her to go to the scene of the crime to try to set her up to find the body. He probably wanted to read about himself in the newspapers. He killed our John Doe and, when the body wasn't found, he set it all up. And then, because he couldn't help himself, he complained about her equipment, which I doubt was shoddy because she seems to know what she's doing. Anyway, I think he may have surfaced early on the dive purposefully so that she would have to swim around looking for him. He was hoping that she would discover the body before the tide changed and she had to make her way to the surface."

"Maybe," Jimmy said. "I guess it's also possible they drowned our victim together and *both* of them wanted to get another look at their handiwork. Now, sensing a breakup, Carla is trying to throw him under the bus."

"This is all a lot of speculation," Lucy said. "And even if you're right about Davis, you need way more evidence because you damn sure won't get a confession out of him."

Austin could always tell when he had a group's attention and when he lost it, and he'd lost Samantha to her laptop. If he'd been a schoolteacher, he would have snapped his fingers to get her attention and forced her to put her laptop in his desk drawer at the front of the classroom. But when Samantha was buried in her laptop, something good usually came of it.

She looked up. "I've got something new. Something potentially big. Well, two things actually." Her computer dinged, and she went silent, apparently reading an email. "Wait, actually three things."

Austin folded his arms and leaned against the wall.

This was going to be good.

CHAPTER SEVENTEEN

SAMANTHA CARRIED her laptop to the front of the room, then plugged it into a long black cable.

She was the quintessential tech prodigy, a blend of brains and casual flair. With her binary code tattoo peeking out from the side of her foot, she was often seen with her bare feet propped up on a desk, dressed in jeans and a Thor t-shirt that matched her no-nonsense attitude. She had been an honors student in criminal justice at Olympic College, specializing in forensic science and digital forensics, but it was her innate understanding of AI, blockchain, and cybersecurity that made her indispensable to the team's investigations.

And Austin always smiled when he saw her carrying her laptop. She held it with the same care one might reserve for a delicate artifact. She had a reverence for technology and its power to uncover hidden truths, one that Austin was slowly—*very* slowly—beginning to share.

The screen on the wall lit up and Austin moved to a seat in the back to get a better view.

"It's rare that three pieces of evidence drop into my

inbox in the same five minutes," she began, "but I think it's a good omen for our day." Her eyes dropped to the laptop screen and she went quiet for a moment as files loaded. "First, let's start with the biggest thing—the one that came in third. The first victim at Deception Pass, Helen Virginia Fullman. About four years ago, her social security checks were flagged. We don't yet have the full report, but we can see that it was flagged with 'suspicious activity.' According to what I'm seeing, the case was never fully investigated due to short staffing and then the fact that she was deceased."

"That's not that unusual that a case would get dropped," Jimmy said. "They are overwhelmed at those offices, and unless there is massive fraud, I could see them sticking something in a drawer once the person is deceased. Does it say what kind of fraud, or who was actually suspected?"

Samantha shook her head. "No. Zero follow-up." She nodded up at the screen, which had finally loaded, showing the name of the victim and the history of her Social Security checks. A red mark showed that on July 7th, 2020, her account had been flagged for suspicious activity. She had received nine checks after that date and then passed away, at which point her account had been closed.

"Okay," Samantha continued, "so that's obviously something with potential. Social security fraud is big business. But we've got a list of six spots that received deliveries of gravel that match the particular blend found on our victims. Apparently, this blend of two different colors of basalt is not that common."

A list popped up on the screen and Austin scanned it. There was nothing unusual or remarkable about any of the locations. One was a trailer park right at the border of Silverdale and Bremerton. Another was a private residential community on Bainbridge Island. The third was a small retailer in Oakville that had bought a supply and then resold it. Austin assumed that's where Ben Davis had gotten his. The rest of the list was more of the same.

Lucy nodded at Jimmy. "My darling husband and I are going to be visiting those spots today, at least as many as we can make it to. After my call, that is. I've got to keep Larsen out of our hair for another few days. I swear it's like that guy has nothing better to do than to make our jobs harder." She shook her head, then waved at Samantha to continue.

"If we get lucky, Lucy and Jimmy will find something at one of the sites that bought that kind of gravel. A suspect or possibly an employee who worked there. Third, I looked into what Austin told me last night, that Ben Davis had mentioned that Carla is an undocumented immigrant and that there's a shady owner of her business. The woman who owns the building is named Stephanie Cooper."

As she spoke, a photograph of Stephanie Cooper popped up on the screen. She appeared to be in her mid-forties with short blonde hair and a sharp nose. She was smiling, but didn't look especially warm.

"I pulled this photo from her Facebook account," Samantha said. "She's a mother of three and has lived on Whidbey Island her whole life. Coupeville. She is actually the legal owner of the dive shop. Carla is essentially a front woman for the business. She's the diving expert, Stephanie Cooper handles all the money and business decisions. It looks like there may have been some faulty business records, though we're not sure. We're going to look into her more. Very possible there's nothing here, but worth digging a little."

Samantha looked around as though waiting for someone to add something.

"That's all well and good," Kendall said, "but I still think it's all about Davis and his shrooms business for the elderly."

Something clicked in Austin's mind. "Wait a second," he said, "go back."

Samantha shrugged. "Go back where?"

"Go back to the list of the Social Security checks received by the first victim."

Samantha tapped a few times, returning to the list of checks.

Austin said, "The address on the top of the file. Pine Woods Trailer Community. Now please click back over to the list of locations that received that type of gravel." The very first location was Pine Woods Trailer Community on the border of Silverdale and Bremerton.

"I see it now," Samantha said. "Helen Fullman's checks were being sent to a home at one of the trailer park communities where the gravel was dropped."

"Twenty bucks says there's a Ben Davis connection there," Kendall said.

Lucy smiled. "Either way, that will be our very first stop. Jimmy and I will head there now. Kendall and Austin, you two are heading to the retirement community to chat with Jack Ulner. Keep in touch."

They all stood at roughly the same time, and Austin followed Lucy out into the hallway. He was about to grab a cup of coffee for the road when he heard a strange metallic reverberation and an unintelligible voice booming from outside of the office.

He raised his head to look out the window. "Oh no," he whispered to himself.

"What the hell?" Lucy exclaimed.

County Commissioner Larsen was standing out front of their office holding a bullhorn, and three news cameras were filming him.

CHAPTER EIGHTEEN

AUSTIN STEPPED out into the cool morning air, met by the bullhorn-amplified pontification of Larsen.

"In multiple states across the country, psychedelics have been legalized or largely decriminalized over the last few years. Now, the so-called law enforcement officers of the Kitsap Sheriff's Department have decided it was a good use of county time and resources to investigate a law-abiding citizen, albeit one who may be operating right at the *edge* of the law, for good and moral purposes.

"Psychedelics, as shown by numerous Harvard and Yale studies, can provide the elderly with much-needed relief both from traumatic experiences and even from pain. Just as Washington state has legalized marijuana, which is now used by over thirty percent of seniors within Kitsap County, I believe we should be legalizing small amounts of all-natural psychedelic products, like those provided by Mr. Davis. And, most importantly, we should not be wasting precious county resources on law enforcement officers locking up well-meaning citizens—who don't even live in our county, by the way—like Mr. Davis."

Austin paced, his frustration growing with each step.

"Furthermore, our newest detective, Thomas Austin, broke into this man's home without a warrant. So not only is he a dangerous and reckless detective, not only is he operating in another county, and not only is he doing so for the purposes of investigating a crime that should be legal, he's doing so without even following protocol."

A photographer snapped a few pictures, and, all the while, cameras were rolling on Larsen. He handed the bullhorn to a woman standing at his side. Gretchen Vale, Davis's attorney.

"As a defense attorney, I have represented many innocent men and women accused of heinous crimes. In this case, I am defending an innocent man accused of a nonheinous crime. The real criminals are inside this building." She paused and dramatically pointed at the Kitsap Sheriff's Department. Then, keeping her finger level, she continued. "They are the ones abusing their power and wasting valuable resources on prosecuting a man who is doing nothing but trying to help our seniors, while the people in this building are using your money trying to do the opposite."

Austin nodded at Kendall and began to make his way across the parking lot. He didn't need to stick around for the rest of this. As he pulled out his keys, he turned, unable to ignore Vale's diatribe.

"Under the doctrine of therapeutic necessity, my client's actions in possessing and distributing small quantities of naturally occurring psychedelic mushrooms to elderly individuals fall squarely within a permissible legal and ethical framework. Given the substantial body of empirical evidence substantiating the medicinal benefits of psilocybin for treating conditions such as chronic pain, PTSD, and end-of-life existential distress, his actions constitute a lawful exercise of compassionate care. Furthermore, pursuant to the precedent established in landmark cases regarding medical cannabis, where state jurisdictions have recognized the preeminence of health and well-being over rigid enforcement of archaic drug statutes..."

Austin slammed the door and Kendall did as well. "I have no idea if every word out of her mouth is BS or not," Kendall said, "but I have a feeling we aren't gonna get much on Davis."

Austin started the car. "Then let's hope Jack Ulner has something interesting to say."

As he pulled out of the driveway, his phone rang with a number he hadn't gotten a call from in quite a while. Anna Downey's name popped up on the console screen.

"Isn't she that reporter?" Kendall asked.

"She is," Austin said.

"Didn't you used to date her?" Kendall asked.

Austin made his face a straight line. "I did."

"Well, aren't you going to answer it?" Kendall asked.

Austin didn't say anything, just tapped the little green phone icon on the console. "Hey, Anna."

"Hey," she said.

"You're on speakerphone," Austin said. "I'm here with Detective Kendall Shaw."

"I'll be brief," Anna said. "I just saw you on TV, well not TV exactly, but they are live streaming the press conference in front of your office. I'm watching it at home."

"Wonderful," Austin said. He usually wasn't one for sarcasm, but the thought of Anna watching him on her laptop as a backdrop to Larsen and Vale's press conference was enough to really piss him off.

"Word is," Anna said, "that they're planning a big vote for next week. Vale is going to be a witness at the County Board of Commissioners meeting. She is going to argue that our police department is bloated and she will bring up examples of times when you folks have overreached and persecuted people wrongly."

"I've been seeing her on the news more and more," Austin said.

"Yeah," Kendall agreed. "I've seen her on CNN a couple times lately and it looks like she is beginning to get a national profile."

"Right," Anna continued. "So, what I'm saying is, people might start to care about issues on her platform. Long story short, she wants to cut the funding of the sheriff's department by forty percent. That would eliminate you, Austin, eliminate Kendall, leave a skeleton crew basically. I know you probably already are, but watch your back."

"Thanks for looking out for us," Kendall said.

"I'm happy to help," Anna said. "You should also know that Vale is a big contributor to Larsen. Fairly sure there is some corruption there but I can't prove it."

Austin wasn't shocked to hear this. "Thanks," he said. "Anything else? I mean, do you know anything else about why they decided to hold this press conference now?"

"I have an idea, but it's potentially libelous for me to speak it out loud," Anna said. "And I realize I have no right to ask but, I do request that these words don't leave your car."

"Our lips are sealed," Kendall said.

She looked over at Austin as if expecting him to say something. But Austin found himself in a bit of a stupor, considering his history with Anna.

"And Austin is nodding, too," Kendall lied.

"Okay then," Anna continued. "Well, Larsen was one of the first to get involved in the marijuana business back when it was first legalized. I wouldn't be shocked to find out that he and Vale are using this Ben Davis thing to drum up sympathy for their cause. Probably want to go into the

psychedelics business together, if they eventually get legalized. In any case, don't believe anything out of Vale's mouth.
She is a damn good attorney, but she usually has an ulterior
motive."

"Thanks," Austin said.

"I gotta go," Anna said. "I hope we can be in touch
again."

Austin ended the call.

"That was... not great," Kendall said.

"You mean how they want to defund half of our
department?"

"No, I meant between you and Anna. I'm guessing it
didn't end well?"

"Eh," Austin said. "Could have been worse." He didn't
want to go into details, but he was glad that the ice between
him and Anna had at least thawed a little.

CHAPTER NINETEEN

MARJORIE "MADGE" Evering looked up and waved a finger in the air to catch the attention of TJ, the friendly aide who always gave her a little extra champagne in her brunch time mimosa. She only allowed herself one, and she didn't want it to be mostly juice.

Madge was eighty years old, but her body still felt sixty and her mind was as sharp as it had been when she'd gotten her PhD in history at age thirty-eight. In her heart, she was still a happy-go-lucky eleven-year-old girl.

She had moved into Seaside Cedars Retirement Community on Bainbridge Island two years ago, soon after her husband had passed away, and hadn't missed a single opportunity for a mimosa.

TJ set down her specially-doctored drink with a wink as the rest of the residents took their seats. Madge sipped her boozy beverage, savoring the extra splash of champagne.

The room buzzed with chatter and laughter as residents filled their plates with brunch delicacies. Madge always ate *after* the trivia; it gave her an advantage to be undistracted by pastries and fruit and eggs. It also allowed for the alcohol to hit her a little stronger, which she enjoyed.

At the front of the room, John, one of the more enthusiastic aides, stood with a stack of trivia questions, ready to entertain the eager crowd. "Alright, everyone, time for the first question!" His voice carried over the hum of the room. "Can everyone finish taking their seats, please?"

At the pace that some of her co-residents moved, this could take a while, Madge thought. She took another sip, watching her neighbors slowly shuffling across the carpet to find their seats.

She was still fully capable of living on her own, but she'd been lonely, and this was the perfect place for her. Not only did they offer *way* more activities and have nicer facilities than most of the places in the county, they also had multiple levels of care. She wasn't going to slow down anytime soon, but she knew it would happen eventually. And when it did, she'd have the nurses and doctors and caregivers and people like TJ at the ready to help her when she would need it most.

For now, she lived in her little one-bedroom apartment, swam in the swimming pool almost every day, and played bingo on Tuesdays.

In her time at Seaside Cedars, she'd organized a charity auction, three canned food drives for various holidays, and even a series of speaker events. Most recently, she'd hosted an author talk with David Dierdrick Zwart, one of her favorite mystery authors. Zwart lived only about forty-five minutes away and wrote a hit series of novels featuring a private investigator and his lovable canine companion solving crimes throughout the region. People had warned her to never meet her heroes, especially her *literary* heroes, as authors were notoriously strange. And in this case, she wished she'd listened. Zwart had been one of the most arrogant, off-putting humans she'd ever come across. Although his books were well-written, well-researched, and full of lovable characters, the man himself was insufferable.

After the event, even TJ, who was always defending everyone and was deeply accepting of *all* people, admitted, "I kind of wish that guy would go the way of one of his victim characters and wash up on a local beach."

TJ had given her an extra splash of Bailey's in her coffee that night, even though he scolded her gently for *being such a lush*. Apparently he was studying to be a physical therapist and acupuncturist and was much more in favor of *natural* medicines. But despite the unpleasant evening, she and TJ shared a laugh and Madge had vowed never to read another of Zwart's novels.

So instead, she'd been focusing on the community's trivia events. And now her favorite part of the week was kicking the crap out of all the other residents in the trivia brunch. She had personally placed it on the activity calendar, and it was now one of the best-attended events in the facility.

Once everyone had found a seat, John began. "Who can tell me which year the Titanic sa—?"

A hand shot up. "1912!" called Mrs. Thompson, a former history teacher with an impressive memory for dates.

Madge had known that one, but Mrs. Thompson's hand had been up before John even finished the question.

"Correct!" John beamed. "Next question: What was the original name of New York City?"

"New Amsterdam," answered Mr. Collins, a retired lawyer who rarely missed a trivia brunch.

"Right again!" John said. "Okay, this one might be a bit tougher. Spiral staircases were built into fire stations to prevent horses from going upstairs where the firefighters slept and kept their food. But why were spiral staircases invented in the first place?"

The room fell quiet as people pondered the question. After thinking for a moment, Madge raised her hand confidently. She hadn't known why spiral staircases were built into fire stations, but she *did* know their original purpose. "In medieval castles, spiral staircases were invented to defend against sword-wielding attackers. The tight, twisting design made it difficult for right-handed intruders to swing their swords effectively as they ascended."

"That's absolutely correct, Madge!" John said. "Well done."

Madge smiled, feeling a warm sense of accomplishment. She took another sip of her mimosa, content to be surrounded by friends and engaged in the activities she loved.

The trivia continued, with questions ranging from ancient civilizations to modern history, and Madge remained sharp, answering several more with ease and enjoying the camaraderie of the group.

She loved her life at Seaside Cedars, and couldn't wait to see what the next year brought.

CHAPTER TWENTY

"I'M JUST SAYING," Jimmy said, "she's your *mother*."

Lucy gripped the steering wheel tight, so tight that her knuckles popped. "And I'm just saying that, because she's my mother, I should be the one who decides whether she moves in with us."

"In *my* family," Jimmy said, "it doesn't matter if we're fighting, or how bad a falling out we've had, or who punched who at last year's Thanksgiving after too many whiskeys. If it's family, you reach out to help them immediately, no questions asked."

Lucy sighed. This was one of the things she loved about Jimmy and his family. In his family, people could get into big fights and disagree about politics or religion or anything else, and somehow they still all came together at the end of the day to have a beer.

Her family was more spread out across the country, not as close. It wasn't that she had had some massive falling out with her mother; she just wanted her own space. So when Jimmy had offered to convert the garage into an apartment for her mom to live in without asking her first, a little hole had formed in the hull of their relationship. The problem was, Lucy couldn't agree to start repairing the leak and Jimmy couldn't bail water fast enough.

She pulled off the road onto a long driveway that led to the trailer park. "We need to get our minds back on this thing, Jimmy. For now, I'll say this: I know it's probably a great idea and we'll end up creating a space and letting her move in. But, did you ever consider that I might not want my mother around close enough to opine about my pancake recipe, or choice of coffee brand, through my kitchen window? I'm in one of the toughest periods of my life, you know that. This new job and are we going to have kids or aren't we? All that stuff. Maybe I don't want my mother's opinion about every little thing I do."

Jimmy said, "But, if we *do* have kids, it will be great that your mother is there. She can help. There's nothing she would like more."

Lucy was exasperated. As usual, he was missing the point. She parked in front of a small brown trailer office and shifted her focus back to their work. "Let's check in there," she said. "Then we'll head back to the address from the Social Security checks."

As Austin pulled into the driveway of the group home where Jack Ulner lived, his console screen lit up. Sy was calling.

"Hey," he said, "I'm just pulling into a location where we need to interview someone, and you're on speakerphone. Kendall is in the car, too."

"Of course, you're at work. I'm sorry I'm interrupting your day." Sy apologized with a soft and sweet voice. "Hey, Kendall."

"Hey, Sy," Kendall answered.

"No worries," Austin said.

"Well," Sy said awkwardly, "we don't need to talk now, but I just wanted to hear your voice."

"I know, me too, and I'm sorry we can't talk much right now." Austin stifled his frustration at their continuing failure over to connect on the phone. They kept missing each other, and now Austin couldn't talk with her.

"No worries, though," Sy said.

"Yes," Austin agreed. "No worries."

Suddenly, Kendall burst out laughing. "You two are too much. I've never met a couple who are more self-effacing and humble. Can you imagine the children you would have? They would be so polite. *No worries, honey. Oh, no worries, dearie.*" Kendall laughed again. "Seriously though, you would have the *nicest* kids ever. I mean, *if* you have kids."

Sy laughed. "You mean *when* we have kids."

This took Austin off guard, but he figured she was probably joking.

Kendall was still running with the joke. "*Oh, we don't need to talk, sweetie,*" she said in a high-pitched voice, mimicking Sy. Then she made her voice deep and hoarse, a poor imitation of Austin's voice. "*No worries. The job comes first, honey.*" Then back in Sy's voice, "*Understood, sweetie pie.*"

"I believe you're taking some poetic license with your rendition of our interaction," Austin said.

"I was simply reading between the lines," Kendall said.

"We can talk later, Sy," Austin said.

"We can try," Sy answered.

"Bye, Kendall," Sy said.

Austin ended the call. "Can we get back to work?"

The building was a charming two-story structure with a wide, wraparound porch, typical of the Pacific Northwest. The exterior was painted a faded but inviting shade of yellow, with white trim that framed the numerous windows. Tall, stately Douglas firs and cedar trees surrounded the property, their branches swaying gently in the morning breeze. The porch had several rocking chairs and small tables, suggesting a place where residents could sit and enjoy the serene surroundings.

The roof was steeply pitched, covered in dark shingles, and the windows on the upper floor had small awnings to shield them from the frequent rain. Flower boxes under each window spilled over with bright red geraniums and trailing ivy, adding a splash of color to the earthy tones of the converted farmhouse. The driveway was gravel—tiny gray pebbles that didn't match the kind found on the victims, Austin noted.

"I don't know about you," Kendall said, getting out of the car, "but to me this feels a bit shady. You know how Ben Davis's mushroom business is kinda skirting the law, at least as his lawyer would like us to believe?"

Austin nodded. "Yeah, this may be one of those semi-legal establishments as well."

In the front yard, a well-tended garden showcased a variety of plants native to the region: rhododendrons, lavender, and clusters of ferns. A wooden bench sat beneath a large maple tree, its leaves providing dappled shade. The air smelled fresh, with a hint of pine and the distant scent of the nearby Sound.

Austin knocked on the door and a woman answered almost immediately. She was in her late thirties or early forties, with short brown hair, round cheeks, and little bags under her eyes.

"We spoke earlier, I believe," Kendall said. "Are you Christine?"

"Yes, please come in," Christine said. "As I mentioned,

I'm the owner's daughter, but I do most of the work around here these days."

"How long has this house been a place of business?" Austin asked.

There was an aroma that permeated the entrance that Austin recognized as artificial ocean smell. It was strong, though not unpleasantly so, with a sweet and briny scent that contained notes of iodine, ozone, and sunscreen. Austin saw an outlet underneath the small guestbook table in the vestibule entrance that had a scent dispenser plugged into it. The little nightlight-shaped object was releasing a steaming plume of what Austin assumed was the fragrance.

"Oh, my mom started the place over fifteen years ago," Christine said, leading them into a little sitting area and offering them the couch, which they both declined. Faint, cheesy elevator music was playing from concealed speakers.

"And what is the legal status of this place?" Kendall asked.

Christine took a deep breath before explaining, "Well, this place originally got an exception about twenty years ago to operate as a bed and breakfast, even though it was zoned residential. When my mom bought it in 2006, she saw an opportunity and decided to turn it into a small retirement community. She went through all the proper channels and got the necessary paperwork and licenses to make it legal as a senior living facility. We're classified as a five-bedroom senior care home, and I'm a certified nursing assistant, so I handle a lot of the day-to-day care. I know it's a bit unusual because of the zoning history, but we've kept everything above board. It's all in the records if you need to check."

"That won't be necessary," Kendall said. "Right now, we would just like to speak with Jack Ulner."

Christine nodded curtly. "I'll be right back."

Kendall gave Austin a look, which he took to mean—*Do you buy her story?*—and Austin shrugged in answer. He didn't know about the ins and outs of the law regarding facilities like this, but the place looked pleasant enough—just as good as some of the facilities he'd seen in the past. Though it was smaller and a bit unusual, the story would probably check out when they looked into it.

A moment later, Christine returned with Jack Ulner by her side. He looked like he was in his late seventies, but could be a healthy eighty-something as well. He was mostly bald with a few straggles of hair over his ears. He wore brown pants, and his white button-down was half tucked into his pants and half hanging out from underneath his belt.

"Are you Jack Ulner?" Austin asked.

"Indeed I am," the man said, a twinkle in his eye.

Austin held up a large plastic bag holding his shoe. "Do you recognize this?"

Ulner leaned forward and inspected the bag. "Damn right I do. Says right there, plain as day, Jack Ulner."

"But, are you sure it's your shoe?" Kendall asked.

"That's my wife's handwriting as sure as I'm living and breathing and as sure as she's still dead and buried," Ulner said. "God bless her soul, may she rest in peace, and may the Lord bless me soon too, as I can't wait to be with her."

Austin felt his chest deflate a bit. "Did someone take them from you then?"

"I don't think so," he said. "Sometimes we donated old shoes, sometimes we gave them away."

"We don't have any record that any of your shoes went missing, do we, Jack?" Christine asked. "They must have been a pair you gave away before you moved here."

"Quite possibly," he said, "And if you're looking to return them, we don't give refunds." Ulner sounded firm on that.

"And do you always label your shoes?" Kendall asked.

"It's not a requirement, but most of our residents do," Christine interjected. "Even though we only have a few people here, sometimes residents have similar shoes, and sometimes people get confused, you know?"

Ulner sat down on the couch and slowly took off one of his loafers. He tried to hand it to Kendall, but she didn't take it, choosing instead to crouch down and look at the inside of it. "His name is there, just like on the one we found," Kendall said. "Different handwriting though."

Ulner nodded in agreement. "I wrote that myself. One you have is an older pair, wife's handwriting."

Austin sat down on the couch and pulled out a notebook. They'd need to get all the details, but if the story checked out, this was just another dead end.

Jack Ulner seemed perfectly believable and, after all, his story made sense. He'd donated his old shoes, another elderly man had picked them up and then later turned up drowned under the Deception Pass Bridge.

Austin let out a long sigh.

They were nowhere.

Lucy and Jimmy found the little blue single-wide trailer under a wide cedar tree toward the back of the trailer park. The man in the office hadn't known whether the owners were home or not, but had confirmed that the place belonged to a man named Terrance Brian Jacoby.

The path leading from the office to the individual trailers had been the same blue and gray basalt that they'd found in the jackets of multiple victims. That confirmed what they already knew, but it was the fact that the Social

Security checks of one of the victims had been sent to this address that had really piqued their interest.

The man in the office had confirmed their suspicions, but not in the way they'd expected. Helen Virginia Fullman had never lived at the address where the Social Security checks had been sent. The odd thing was that she *had* lived at another address in the same trailer park. They'd decided to start with the address to which the checks had been sent.

Jimmy nodded and rapped on the thin glass window on the door of the trailer.

"Be on the ready," Lucy said. "This could get messy."

A moment later, the door swung open, and Jimmy was struck by the scent of freshly baked cookies. A man stood there, roughly forty years old, wearing a white apron and crisp jeans. He had shaggy blond hair, a handsome face, and an affable if slightly dull smile.

"Can I help you?" he asked.

"Are you Mr. Jacoby?" Jimmy asked.

"Sure am."

"Do you know anything about a woman named Helen Virginia Fullman?"

Lucy watched his face carefully as it contorted slightly.

He let out a long sigh. "I knew this would come back up at some point," he said, his voice tinged with exasperation. "You're with the Kitsap Sheriff's Department?"

Jimmy nodded.

Lucy was trying to get a read on the guy, who seemed perfectly pleasant, like he'd been expecting this visit.

"I'm happy to come in with you and talk about it," he said. "You should grab my neighbor, too." He pointed toward a bright yellow trailer across the path. "His name is Forest. I'm not sure if he's home right now, but together we can explain the whole situation." He turned. "But first lemme get these cookies out of the oven.

CHAPTER TWENTY-ONE

IT WAS rare that the team had two important witnesses in the building at the same time, but, by around noon, that's exactly what was happening.

Austin finished his sandwich standing up in the hallway and tossed the wrapper into a small garbage can.

"Who do you want to start with?" Lucy asked him.

Before he could answer, Kendall said, "Let's start with Ben Davis. I still think he's our guy, although I have to admit the evidence is pointing in Jacoby's direction."

Jimmy joined them in the hallway, holding a cup of coffee. To their left, Ben Davis was in Conference Room A, sitting with his lawyer, Gretchen Vale. She was fresh off her news conference and seemed ready to go to war for her shroom-dealing client.

To their right, in Conference Room B, Terrence Brian Jacoby sat next to his neighbor Forest and Forest's attorney Kenny Smith. Chatting and sipping sodas, the three appeared to want nothing more than the opportunity to clear this up. They'd learned that Forest was actually Forest

Fullman, a nephew of the woman found at Deception Pass three years earlier, Helen Virginia Fullman.

Lucy said, "Austin, you lead the interview with Davis. Kendall, you just stare at him, see if you can get a rise out of the bastard. Jimmy and I will go chat with our social security fraudsters."

Austin nodded and headed into Conference Room A, taking a seat across from Vale. Kendall stood in the corner as directed, arms folded. Davis struck Austin as the kind of guy who would feel bad about not being able to outrun a woman. Despite being older and out of shape and up against Kendall, who looked like she could probably make the Olympic pole vaulting team, Davis seemed like a fragile and shallow man. He hoped Kendall's icy stare would make him lose his cool, make him say something he shouldn't. Though with Vale there, he doubted it.

"So, Ben," Austin began, keeping his tone casual, "let's talk about what happened on the day of the dive."

Vale immediately cut in, "My client has already told you everything he knows."

"Humor me," Austin said, leaning back in his chair. "We just want to make sure we have the details straight."

Ben shifted uncomfortably in his seat. "I already told you. Carla and I went for a dive. She found the body. I didn't even know about it until later. When she got out of the water she seemed upset but—get this—not about having just seen a corpse like you're telling me, she was upset *at me,* for exiting the water without proper communication. If she found a corpse it didn't faze her much, the way I see it."

"You know," Austin said, "it's strange how you pushed to go diving exactly where the body was. Almost like you knew it was there. And stranger still that the rocks found in the coat of the victim match the ones in your driveway."

Ben's face reddened. "Ever heard of coincidence? I didn't even know we had been swimming with a cadaver."

Vale leaned forward, her voice sharp. "Detective Austin, unless you have new evidence to present, you're just wasting our time." She offered a sarcastic smile. "But I guess that's what this department specializes in. An issue our beloved public will be weighing in on soon."

Austin almost took the bait, but he managed to keep his mouth closed. He glanced at Kendall, who hadn't moved a muscle.

"Why push to dive at Deception Pass?" Austin asked.

"Sure," Ben said. "Always wanted to dive Deception Pass. It's known to have some of the most beautiful wildlife and coral in the region. And yeah, I wanted to date Carla because I knew she was an expert, or at least I *thought* she was before she gave me that crappy equipment. Before her, I'd only been on a few dives. What I didn't know was that she was illegal and a total 'B.'"

Kendall slowly moved forward and put her palms face down on the table, leaning her long frame across it toward Davis. "Does it make you feel good to call a woman that just because she doesn't like you?"

"It would make me feel good to call you that right now," he said.

"Then do it," Kendall said.

Austin watched them stare each other down, neither speaking.

Finally, Vale interjected, "Detective Kendall, I don't know how you guys did things in Los Angeles, and, judging by your crime rates, you didn't do a very good job there either. Here, in Washington state, we don't barge into citizens' homes for legally gathering a few mushrooms that may or may not end up having some psychedelic properties to them. He also enjoyed gathering chanterelles if that matters to you."

"I make a mean mushroom Bolognese," Ben said. "I'm a vegan."

"You *would* be a vegan," Kendall said.

Austin touched Kendall on the arm, nudging her away from Davis. "It doesn't matter what anyone here eats. What matters is the deceased man whom your client was only a few feet from and claims not to have seen. A man weighed down by gravel that matches the gravel in his driveway."

"If you ask me," Ben said, folding his arms and plastering a smug look across his face, "you should be looking more into Carla and Carla's silent partner. She's got a nasty reputation."

Lucy brushed a curl off her forehead as she sat across from Kenny Smith, a young attorney who represented Jacoby's neighbor, Forest.

Both Forest and Jacoby were on their second cans of soda and looked pretty amped up.

Lucy decided to start with Jacoby. "You told Detective Jule and me that there was a perfectly reasonable explanation for the fact that Social Security checks were sent to your address even though the recipient did not live there. We're all ears."

Jimmy sat next to her, setting down his cup of coffee forcefully. He seemed to be trying to intimidate them, but, Lucy thought, he just looked like a fool. The coffee splashed out because it was too full, and he burned his hand. He shook off the pain with a grimace.

Normally, a suspect would make some comment or

laugh. But, Lucy had to admit to herself, these people seemed like decent guys eager to get the truth out there.

"If I may," the lawyer began, "I already know all the ins and outs of this case because we first worked on it a few years back."

"I don't care who gives it," Lucy said, "but I want an explanation."

The lawyer cleared his throat. "Alright, here's the situation. About four years ago, Forest had his mailbox bashed in by vandals."

"Couple punk kids," he said, "and that's when everything went wrong."

CHAPTER TWENTY-TWO

"THE MAILBOX THING wasn't just a one-time incident," Smith continued. "It kept happening. Now, Forest's aunt, whom you mentioned was found deceased under Deception Pass Bridge around three years ago, lived with him at the time. That's why the Social Security checks were initially being sent to his address. They shared the same residence." He leaned forward, emphasizing his point. "The trailer park, which, to be honest, has terrible maintenance, wouldn't replace the damn mailbox. There was this ongoing fight over who was going to pay for it—the park management or Forest. Meanwhile, the aunt needed her checks and other important mail to arrive reliably, so, for a while, they had everything rerouted to Mr. Jacoby's address because they were pals. It was just across the walkway at the trailer park. It seemed like a simple and effective solution."

He paused to let that sink in before continuing. "Now, every time the checks came in, Ms. Fullman would sign them over to Forest because he was paying all the bills. They had this understanding. So, yes, the checks were being flagged for having an odd address when they were re-routed to Mr. Jacoby's home, but if you look at it, it's right across the walkway. This was all on the up and up. The Social Security office flagged it, which makes sense from a bureaucratic standpoint, but there was nothing illegal or shady going on. They were just trying to manage in a place that wasn't providing the basic maintenance they were paying for."

He leaned back, giving Lucy and Jimmy a look that was both earnest and slightly weary. "If you check the records and talk to the folks around here, you'll see it's exactly as I'm telling you. Just a case of neighbors helping each other out in a housing community that doesn't always look out for its residents."

"What's your understanding of how she died?" Jimmy asked Forest. "Your aunt, that is."

"Truly believe it was an accident, wild as she was," Forest said, his voice heavy. "Aunt Helen had disappeared for weeks at a time before. Usually just traveling. So when she disappeared that last time, we kept depositing checks thinking she would come back. After all, we were paying her credit card and all her bills and whatnot. When we found out that she had died a couple weeks earlier, we were shocked." He folded his hands in his lap.

Smith added, "They paid back the Social Security checks that had been inadvertently deposited after she died, and the case was closed. It wasn't shoved in a drawer or anything; it was closed because nothing actually went wrong."

"And the rocks?" Lucy asked. "What might they have been doing in her pockets? And why was she out on Whidbey Island?"

Forest grimaced, shaking his head. "First question, I don't know. She was an odd duck toward the end. Second question, well, she explored all over, and she was still driving at the time."

"Police looked into Forest as a suspect," Smith said, "but only briefly before ruling it an accident. He provided his whereabouts and that was that."

"Roofing contractor conference," Forest interjected. "I'm the best in Kitsap if you ever need a new roof." He shook his head, apparently embarrassed. "Anyway, what happened to my Aunt was tragic. She was losing her grip on reality and shouldn't have been driving. Lord knows how she ended up on that bridge."

Jimmy, who had been listening intently, held up his phone in front of Lucy. It was the same list of Social Security checks Samantha had shown them the previous day. Like they'd all claimed, it showed that the Social Security checks had only been flagged when the address had been changed from Forest's to Jacoby's. Their story matched the evidence perfectly.

"Please excuse us," Lucy said, standing.

Austin had heard just about enough from Ben Davis.

He was beginning to believe that Davis had nothing to do with this particular crime, but Austin didn't doubt that he was capable of crimes worse than selling psychedelic mushrooms to senior citizens.

When they heard a gentle *tap tap tap* on the door, he excused himself. Three taps meant Lucy wanted to talk. Kendall followed Austin out into the hall, where Lucy explained the ins and outs of how the Social Security checks had been fraudulently deposited.

"What do you think of his story?" Austin asked.

Lucy considered this. "I mean, their story checks out, I

guess, but it's a hell of a coincidence that our first victim also had Social Security checks, not stolen but, well, sort of fraudulently deposited."

"The truth is," Jimmy said, "it's not that uncommon. A lot of relatives take care of their elderly family members who sign over Social Security checks or have their family cash the checks for them. It's just part of how the world works. And it makes sense that the victim would have the gravel in her pockets because if she had memory issues, she could have shoved them in there. Part of me thinks Fullman *may* have been an accident, and that still wouldn't rule out that our other two could be murders. What a mess."

"How's it going with Davis?" Lucy asked.

Kendall frowned. "I don't know what it is about that guy. I can't put my finger on his guilt around this, and now I'm thinking he's not guilty of drowning anyone, but I wouldn't mind facing off against him in a steel cage."

Lucy chuckled.

"I don't think he's our guy either," Austin said.

"We will have to let Forest and Jacoby go," Lucy said. "We will check out their story, but..." Lucy's face suddenly flushed red and she slapped the wall with an open palm. After an awkward silence, she turned back to the group. "I'm sorry. Just frustrated. We need to come up with something real."

"You're turning into Ridley more and more every day," Austin said. "I used to think that his face looked like a tea kettle about to boil over when he was getting frustrated."

"Maybe you need some of Davis's psychedelic mushrooms," Jimmy said.

"What?" Lucy shot a death glare at Jimmy.

"You know," Jimmy continued, "go dance to some Grateful Dead in the forest, kind of chill out."

"Don't start with me," Lucy said. "You don't want me chilling out when I go down to visit you in the morgue."

Austin was about to head back in to continue the interview with Davis, but Samantha interrupted, hurrying down the hall. "We got back the analysis on the gravel," she said. "It's not a match."

"Not a match for what?" Austin asked. "Which one?"

"We have confirmed with certainty that the gravel in the victim's pockets *does* all come from the same shipment of basalt. But the gravel in Davis's driveway *doesn't* match. Looks similar, but isn't."

Austin's shoulders slumped. "And the gravel from the trailer park?"

"That matches the shipment."

"And even that may just be a coincidence," Kendall said. "We're going to have to let Davis go, aren't we?"

Lucy nodded. "He can still face charges on the drug crime, maybe resisting arrest. But that's going to be up to the prosecutor, and we're not going to be able to hold him."

Austin wanted to strike the wall just as Lucy had, but he kept his cool.

He had to go back in and tell Ben Davis he was free to go.

CHAPTER TWENTY-THREE

KENDALL'S PRESENCE was clearly not going to intimidate either the lawyer or Davis himself, so Austin had convinced her to watch the next part of the interview on a laptop so he could have Davis all to himself. Since they recorded all the interviews anyway, she could watch it live through a system Samantha had set up.

"Where's the 'B'?" Davis said as Austin sat back down.

Austin clenched his fists, although this time he wasn't close to taking the bait. He was just going to ignore him.

"Don't call her that again," Austin said, his voice calm but firm. "It's not going to help your case or make you look like a tough guy."

"I tell them like I see them," Davis said.

"I need to tell you," Austin said, "and it pains me to do so, the gravel in your driveway is not actually a match for the gravel found on the victims."

A sarcastic grin passed over Vale's face. "So another thing this office has gotten wrong. Not that it mattered, because we already knew my client had nothing to do with this, but I'm glad I now have another reason to make you guys look like fools in the press. By the time I'm through with you, Austin, you'll be back to flipping pancakes and inventing new burgers at your little café. By the way, I was there two weeks ago. And let's just say I won't be dining there ever again."

Austin placed his hands on the table. "Mr. Davis is free to go. He's no longer a suspect in this case, although he will have to answer for the misdemeanor drug charges, as well as resisting arrest."

"What's next?" Davis said, standing. "Bring me back in here on jaywalking charges as I walk away from the building?"

"Thank you," Vale said, "but there's something else I need to tell you now." She slid a phone across the desk.

Austin stared at it, but didn't pick it up. "What's this for?"

"It's unlocked," Vale said. "Please read the text messages there."

Austin started at the top, his insides twisting the further through the chat he got.

Carla: Hey adventurer! 😊

Ben: Hey yourself. I was just dreaming about my next dive.

Carla: So, not dreaming about me then?

Ben: Uh, okay. Jealous much? I bet you're dreaming about your next dive too.

Carla: Guilty. 🐚

Ben: Can't believe you run a dive shop, sounds like a dream job.

Carla: It really is. 🐚 You got me talking about diving when we met and I never asked, what do you do?

Ben: I provide alternative medicine to seniors. Mushrooms, herbal stuff. Trying to help people feel better but not with the stuff that dopes them out, right? I deal with nature's medicines.

Carla: That's so cool! I love that you're into natural remedies. Ever tried diving as a remedy?

Ben: Haha, sure I dive often.

Carla: Oh really? Where's your favorite dive spot?

Ben: There are so many.

Carla: Ever been under Deception Pass Bridge?

Ben: Been meaning to.

Carla: Let's dive it! Let's dive it! Let's dive it!

Ben: No can do. I left my gear with my buddy in Cali. Didn't think I'd face the frigid waters up here anytime soon.

Carla: I'll provide the equipment. Dive shop, remember. It would be a great first date.

Ben: Oh yeah, your dive shop. The tides are crazy there though right?

Carla: What are you a seachicken?

Ben: No such thing... but no. I'm not a seachicken or a seacucumber or a sea-anything.

Carla: That's funny. But I am going to need you to prove it.

Ben: OK OK OK. Let's dive it!

Carla: Oh, you're a shark then are you? We'll see about that. Trust me, you'll love it. And besides, all great loves start in the water. Just like humanity did.

Ben: Haha, that's poetic.

Carla: Can't wait! I promise you, I'll show you something you'll never forget.

Ben: I'm sure you will!

Austin sat down the phone and leveled his eyes at Ben. "Why didn't you tell us from the beginning that it was her idea to go on that dive?"

"Please allow me to answer that," Vale said. "Do you

know who the only person is who's been playing you worse than you've been playing yourself, Detective Austin?"

She smiled. "Me. We were going to have your department for lunch in either case, but you are making this way too easy. And I encourage you to go over the transcript. My client never stated that it was his idea to take that dive."

Austin stood. Assuming this chat was real, they'd been played from the beginning. The only thing is, he had no idea why.

Why would Carla lie about it being Ben's idea to go on that dive? Why would she admit to being there and give them the video but not want them to know it was her idea that they went in the first place?

Nothing was adding up, and Austin was getting more frustrated by the minute. "We will be looking into the authenticity of that text chain," he said.

"Hit us with your best shot," Ben said. "I've given my lawyer permission to have the dating app release the official transcript. It'll all check out. And, by the way, as my lawyer pointed out, I never *actually* said it was my idea to go to Deception Pass. You thought it was, assumed it was, and I let you guys go down that path. It's a policy of mine: when law enforcement officers want to make asses of themselves, let them."

Austin clenched his jaw, but kept his composure.

Vale smirked. "In the meantime detective, unless you have any more baseless accusations, my client will be leaving."

Austin nodded curtly. "Mr. Davis is free to go. But don't get too comfortable. We'll be watching closely."

Ben stood, a smug grin plastered on his face. "I know how to cross the street," he said sarcastically, walking out with Vale.

As the door closed behind them Austin slowly

unclenched his fists, then headed out into the break room to find Kendall.

"You saw?" he asked.

"Nice work, New York." Her tone was peppier than he expected, peppier than he felt.

"You didn't do much better, L.A. And why do you sound so upbeat?"

"Because in this job you're bound to screw up a lot, but we can always bounce back. Plus, I called an officer I know in Oak Harbor to go make contact with Carla. She lied to us. I want to know why and we'll soon find out."

Kendall's phone buzzed on the table. "Ah, it's him already." She tapped the phone, leaving it on the table. "Leo, you're on speakerphone. I'm here with Austin. You found Carla? We can be out there in a couple hours."

"No." A tired voice came through the speakerphone. "Spoke with a girl named Missy, a teenager. She's the dive shop's only employee. Apparently she only works the slow shifts, maybe twenty hours a week average."

"And?"

"Carla didn't turn up for work today."

"What do you mean?" Kendall asked.

"I mean she's not here," he said. "No one can reach her. She's missing."

CHAPTER TWENTY-FOUR

MADGE HAD ALWAYS WANTED to go to Alaska.

In fact, she had begged her husband for years to take the trip. At one point, she'd even gotten flyers from a cruise company and made reservations using his credit card. But he'd insisted that they should use their vacation money to go somewhere warm. "If we have to live in the cursed Pacific Northwest," he'd said, "and endure months of gray, I'm using my vacations to go to Florida or Hawaii, California or Arizona, or damn near anywhere that's sunny."

Finally, after years of shutting down the idea of an Alaska cruise, he'd relented and Madge had set it up. A week later, he'd been diagnosed with stage four brain cancer. He'd passed away six months later, before taking the trip.

But now, Madge had ten days booked on the Alaska Dreamliner, a luxury ship on which she would have a first-class cabin along with two of her best friends from college with whom she'd stayed in touch. They planned this mini-reunion over the last six months, and she'd never been looking forward to a trip more.

The whole trip would be done in luxury. Door-to-door car service from her retirement community on Bainbridge Island to the ferry, where they would drive on and eventually drop her right at the boarding area for the cruise ship.

The car pulled up right on time, a black Lincoln. No regular taxi for her. The driver, a woman who looked vaguely familiar, got out and stowed her luggage before helping her into the car.

As expected, a half bottle of Veuve Clicquot champagne was chilling in bucket of ice in the back, complete with a single champagne glass.

"Just opened it five minutes ago," the driver said. "As instructed."

Madge poured herself half a glass, content to waste the rest. After all, this might be the last major trip she took, and she was going to love every moment of it.

The ferry was only about ten minutes from the facility, though there was a bit of a backup this morning, and by the time they pulled onto the ferry, she'd finished her champagne.

"Will you stay in the car, ma'am?" the driver asked.

"Yes," she said, and her voice sounded odd to her. She was feeling a bit strange. Woozy. She caught the driver looking at her in the rearview mirror.

"Are you feeling alright?" she asked.

"No," she heard herself say, and her voice sounded like she was drunk. But she'd had only half a glass.

"I think I need to use the restroom," Madge said.

The driver didn't say anything, but turned around, studying Madge closely.

Where did she recognize her from? Had she been a volunteer at her facility? Or... She couldn't place her, and her thoughts were now moving slow as molasses in winter.

Madge tried to reach for the door handle, but her arm

wouldn't move. She tried to kick her foot, but it wouldn't move either. Who was the woman? Who was the driver? Why couldn't she move? What was happening?

Madge tried to scream, to speak, to make a noise, anything, but her voice wouldn't come. Everything was growing dark around her, then darker still.

She tried to keep her eyes open, but couldn't.

And as they closed and the last bit of consciousness faded, all she could think was, *Who was the driver, and what the hell was going on?*

CHAPTER TWENTY-FIVE

AFTER LETTING ALL their suspects go, Kendall had convinced Austin they needed a few hours to clear their heads and discuss the case. It was finally time to get their pups together again.

So he'd returned home and picked up Run, then headed back out for a day at the beach.

But now Kendall was the one running late. Austin sat on a weathered log, looking out at Seabeck's Scenic Beach State Park. The sun was shining brightly, casting a golden hue over the landscape. From his vantage point, he could see the wide expanse of sandy shore meeting the gentle waves of Hood Canal. The water sparkled like a sea of diamonds under the clear blue sky. Nearby, clusters of families and groups of friends were scattered about, setting up picnic blankets and beach umbrellas, their laughter and chatter blending with the rhythmic sound of the waves.

Tall evergreen trees bordered the beach, their branches swaying slightly in the warm breeze. A few seagulls soared overhead, their calls punctuating the air. The grassy area adjacent to the beach was dotted with wildflowers in full bloom, and the scent of saltwater mixed with the sweet fragrance of the flowers, creating a blend that made Austin take a deep, contented breath.

Run had been tugging against her leash since they'd arrived, eager to explore. Finally she lay down to nap in the sand as Austin pulled out his phone and called Sy.

"Good timing," she said, answering after only one ring.

"Hey," he said. "Long time no talk. I feel like we're becoming text pen pals or something."

"I've got good news though," she said. "I got final approval. I'll be fully retired in a month, with half my pension and the freedom to do anything I want."

Austin looked out at the water. She sounded so positive about it. He loved that about her. Sometimes he felt a darkness pass through him or even settle on top of him. It didn't happen as much as it did before he solved Fiona's murder, but it still came from time to time. She was a good antidote to that.

"I'm very happy for you," he said.

"So what do you think?"

"Think about what?" Austin asked.

"About me moving out there."

"You know how I feel about that," Austin said. He'd already told her he was thrilled with the idea.

"I want to hear you say it again," she said, "just for fun."

"I would love it if you moved out here."

"Don't worry, I won't try to move in with you," she said. "I'm going to get my own place. I'll be interning two days a week at a winery in central Washington."

Austin watched a seagull land on a log, look side to side, then take off again. "That's a heck of a commute."

"It is," Sy said, "but they have a house on the property with a garage and a little apartment over it that I can stay in when I'm there. It'll be a great learning experience. And I'm starting a local wine club with Claire Anderson."

That surprised Austin; he hadn't known that the two of them were even in touch. "That sounds interesting."

"She's a hoot," Sy said. "Plus, it'll be good to have a girl-friend so it doesn't look like I'm just moving out there for the handsome and charming seaside detective."

"The other day," Austin said, finally gathering the courage, "when you said 'when we have kids,' were you serious?"

"I don't know," Sy replied. "Were you?"

"Was I serious?" Austin asked, confused. "I'm not the one who said it."

"Yeah, I was just trying to bide my time a little bit."

Austin smiled and stood when Run started tugging at her leash again. Kendall was coming toward the beach with her own corgi, Ralph. Run's excitement could no longer be contained.

"I have to go," Austin said. "Kendall is here."

"You two aren't having an affair, are you?" Sy asked, a hint of mirth in her voice.

"I think you know me to be a very loyal person," Austin said. "And you've never struck me as a jealous one."

"I know," Sy said. "I didn't mean it. I mean, I know you're not. I was... well, I guess I was embarrassed about what I said about having kids. I didn't want you to think I was pressuring you or anything, and... well, oh wait, hold on. You have to go, and I'm getting a call from my lawyer about the settlement for my retirement. Let's talk later, okay?"

She didn't wait for his reply. The call went dead.

~

Taking off eastward along the beach, Austin and Kendall talked over the case some, but after coming up with nothing new, Kendall suggested they walk in silence for a while and take in the scenery, which was fine by Austin.

He was distracted anyway. He did believe that Sy had been joking about having kids, but suspected the joke had contained a kernel of truth. She was in her late thirties, Austin in his mid-forties. He knew that if Sy ever *did* want to have kids, there was no time to waste. So her joke had likely been a subtle hint about what she might want for her future.

After walking a considerable distance away from the parking lot, Austin and Kendall found themselves in a more secluded part of Scenic Beach State Park. The hustle and bustle of the populated area had faded away, leaving behind only the peaceful sounds of nature.

The beach here was narrower, with smooth pebbles replacing the sand. The water lapped gently at the shore, and the sunlight filtered through the canopy of trees, casting dappled shadows on the ground. The only sounds were the soft rustle of leaves and the occasional splash of a fish breaking the surface of the water.

They let the dogs off the leash and both took off like they were training for the corgi races that took place at occasional halftime shows during Seahawks games.

Continuing their walk, they moved around a little cove, past a community center and a conference center. The forested area around them was lush and vibrant, with ferns and undergrowth adding to the dense greenery. The air was cooler here, carrying the fresh scent of pine and earth. Austin spotted a deer grazing quietly in the distance, its ears twitching as it listened for any signs of danger.

"Oh no," Kendall said. "The dogs."

She was already hurrying toward the shore, where the dogs were rolling in a massive kelp pile.

The moment the dogs saw Kendall running towards them, they took off down the beach.

Austin followed. "Run!" he called after her.

She ignored him, happily following Ralph.

"I think your dog may be a bad influence on Run," Austin said, nearly catching up with Kendall.

"C'mon," she called over her shoulder. "Live a little.

"Run, come back here!" Austin yelled.

Kendall was laughing breathlessly, finding some humor in the absurdity of the situation. "At least they didn't see that deer."

"Right," Austin agreed.

The chase continued, the dogs pausing just long enough to let their humans think they had a chance of catching up, only to dart off again, a comedic dance of near captures and sudden escapes.

They reached an area near the woodline where there was a particularly clay-rich and muddy bluff. The dogs must have smelled something interesting or liked the way that the cool muddy substance felt over their fur because they both immediately jumped and rolled in the muck with absolute delight.

When Kendall closed in on them this time, they sprinted away in unison, looking like two identical short legged lumps of grayish-brown mess. Austin couldn't for the life of him tell Ralph from Run underneath their muddy disguises.

Finally, the dogs reached a small marina where a woman wearing a white sun dress was just leaving through the gate. Not wanting to be stained by the full-blown *corg-tastrophes,* she stepped aside, allowing the two dogs past the entrance and onto the pier.

"Sorry about this!" Austin called out as he and Kendall followed the dogs onto the dock and jogged down the pier to the boat. Austin smelled smoke, BBQ smoke, and followed the dogs toward it.

Ralph and Run made it to the end of the dock and, without hesitation, leaped onto a boat where a middle-aged couple looked up from their steak-covered grill.

"Sorry," Austin called.

"I'll come grab them," Kendall said, stopping a few feet from the boat.

"Don't worry about it," the man said, flipping a T-bone. "Y'all come right aboard. I guess they must have smelled something good!"

The look on the woman's face did not share the same welcome, and she sat her beer on the cabin top, out of reach of the chaos, before going below deck.

Run sat politely, looking up at the grill-master, while Ralph offered sharp barks between turning tight circles next to Run to prove he was capable of steak-worthy tricks.

The woman returned with a mop and a large towel. Looking like she was waiting for the storm on short legs to pass, she stood at the ready to repair the muddy mess.

While climbing onto the deck of the boat, Austin heard an unfriendly bark, then another.

"That's Milo," the woman said. "That dog's fit to be tied."

"Oh, speak for yourself Millie," the man said. "That dog's all hat and no cattle."

"He means all bark and no bite," the woman said.

Austin smiled and nodded, then turned toward the barking and saw Milo, wedged between the lifelines and leaning against them hard, held back by the girth of his specially-made-for-dogs orange life jacket. His head was sticking out over the water, jowls dripping with slime, barking relentlessly at the canine stowaways a boat away from him.

Ralph moved like lightning when he saw the source of the noise. And thinking he could jump between the boats to face off against Milo, Ralph went to take the leap. But Austin's reflexes were on point. He cut Ralph off before he could make it to the stanchions behind the seating area. Grabbing the filthy animal out of lower mid-air, Austin hugged Ralph to his chest.

Stepping backwards away from the boat edge with Ralph in his arms, Austin stumbled over a loose tackle box, his feet tangling in its contents.

He fell backward, successfully protecting the dog, but striking his head *hard* on the edge of a boat cleat.

Austin's vision blurred.

The world around him was darkening.

The last thing he heard was Kendall's frantic voice calling his name as everything went black.

CHAPTER TWENTY-SIX

AUSTIN WASN'T sure how long he'd been unconscious, and he hadn't known that he could dream while out like a light. But as he came to, with Kendall taking a cold washcloth to his face, he remembered every vivid detail.

After hitting his head and going unconscious, he'd had flashes of many childhood memories. He again thought of burying his father's feet at the beach, but this time he felt like he was actually there again. He again experienced the first time he'd tasted clam chowder at a little café in Bremerton, and felt he could still taste and feel the pillowy texture of the creamy soup.

He watched surfers on a beach in San Diego. And, reliving a time when he lived in Connecticut, he went to both a Red Sox game and a Yankees game on the same day. The Red Sox had been playing an afternoon game, and the moment it had ended, he and his dad drove all the way to New York City to catch a night game at Yankee Stadium. There was no reason to do so. It was just something his dad had wanted to do, and of course, Austin had been thrilled to go along for the ride.

And in all the memories, strangely, a baby boy was there. Austin had never had a brother and, halfway through the dream, he realized the only explanation for the baby being there was that it was his son.

A sense of alarm hit him as though, while eating his mug of chowder, he'd all of a sudden bitten into a piece of clam shell. He was terrified for the baby and had a deep desire to protect him, but he was also terrified for himself. How did he become a twelve-year-old boy, sitting in Yankee Stadium with a child to raise?

There was no explanation for it in the dream, but as he slowly drifted back from unconsciousness, he realized that the kid had black hair like Sy.

He'd also had dreams about others, and these had been less visceral, more of a painting in black and white and sepia tones. He realized he was imagining the childhoods of the victims, long before Austin himself was alive.

Finally, his dad had wafted through his consciousness, sitting at Evergreen Memory Care in Seattle. One moment confused, another moment not, but not able to communicate his thoughts or dreams or desires except in rare moments of lucidity that didn't last long.

"Austin, are you okay?" Kendall asked. "It looks like you're waking up."

Austin blinked and squinted against the glare that surrounded Kendall's face as she looked down at him from above. "I think I'm okay," he said.

"You rang your bell pretty good," a man with a Southern accent said. The boat owner.

Austin felt Run crawl next to him, her wet and muddy body pressing into him. He thought she was making sure he was okay, but he wouldn't put it past her to just be rubbing herself against him to use his body to dry off.

Austin blinked rapidly.

He thought of what a ninety-year-old person's life might be like. How many eras they'd been through—wars and presidents and technologies and even different personal identities. For a long time, Austin's identity had been NYPD detective, husband to Fiona, Assistant District Attorney for Manhattan. He'd assumed that would always be his life.

Then, and he could only see this in retrospect, he'd been on the run.

He'd run all the way to Hansville, vowing never to get involved in police work again. His identity became something new and unfamiliar. Then it changed again after he'd solved the murder of Fiona. For the first time, he felt like he might forge an entirely new path.

He just had no idea what that path was.

Run licked his hand, and this helped bring him to full and present consciousness.

Austin looked up at Kendall. "We need to get back to work."

CHAPTER TWENTY-SEVEN

"THE FIRST THING we need to do," Austin said, "is locate Carla. And to do that, we need to get in touch with the owner of the store."

They had gone straight from the beach back to the office. Thankfully, both Ralph and Run were tuckered out, and after a blast from the outdoor hose behind the station and a nice bowl of water and plenty of treats, they were sleeping soundly in the corner of the room. Run had allowed Ralph the throne's perch of the makeshift bed Austin had made them using a crumpled blanket, and she lay with her neck draped over the side of it, her chin resting against Ralph's shoulder.

They'd gotten in touch with Sheriff Derby, who had been unable to locate Carla or the dive shop's legal owner. Although Carla was a well-known and respected member of the community, the store owner was a bit of a recluse—an odd woman who was not publicly a part of any business, although she had her fingers in three or four, including the dive shop.

Kendall said, "Do you know how much it will piss me

off if it turns out that that bastard Ben Davis was right? If Carla or the owner of the store had anything to do with this..." She trailed off, shaking her head.

Austin thought back to their brief meeting with Carla and the intense black cat. She presented as genuinely afraid and concerned, and the way the video had unfolded made it seem very unlikely that she could have had anything to do with the death of the still unidentified Seabee.

Kendall seemed to be considering the same thing. "I worked a case in Los Angeles once where this man had a split personality. He had killed his wife and stashed the body, then went about his daily life for three days, like nothing happened. *Situation normal.* At the end of the third day, he returned to the crime scene and called in the murder. The call made it sound like he was truly panicked. The police found him there, and he was shocked that they suspected him. Turned out we had an airtight case against him. Strangest thing I ever saw."

Austin considered this. "Do you mean like there were two parts of him? One that was a cold-blooded killer and one that didn't know what he'd done?"

"I'm no psychologist," Kendall replied, "but that's the way a number of shrinks explained it to us. And the jury and judge agreed—no death row. He's in a psychiatric prison for the rest of his life."

Austin shook his head. "Wait, California has the death penalty?"

"They have it," Kendall said. "But, executions are currently on hold indefinitely."

Austin had taped photos of the crime scenes all along the whiteboard, and they'd spent the last half hour revisiting every aspect of the case. Jimmy and Lucy had gone out to the Manette Bridge to take a closer look at the scene in person.

Kendall looked down at her phone. "Good news. I just got a text from Sheriff Derby. He located the store's legal owner and got her to agree to a sit-down interview. He's gonna patch us in via Zoom."

The text contained a link, and Austin immediately excused himself to go find Samantha. Ten minutes later, the Zoom was set up on the screen on the wall, with one of Samantha's laptops acting as a camera. Kendall and Austin sat shoulder to shoulder in front of it.

Sheriff Derby was already there, and, a moment later, Stephanie Cooper, the legal owner of the dive shop joined them. After Sheriff Derby informed her that this would be recorded and was an official police interview, he asked a series of questions establishing her relationship to the dive shop and to Carla.

Next he asked a series of questions regarding the victims and the discoveries of the bodies. Cooper claimed to have no connection to any of them and said she could provide them with solid alibis.

To Austin, it sounded like a fairly common case of a new immigrant partnering with someone who had established money in a community to run a business based on their expertise. But it did lead him to a question.

"Mrs. Cooper, is there any chance Carla is undocumented?"

She didn't say anything at first, but the look on her face said it all.

Sheriff Derby said, "Let me throw this out there. You met Carla at some point before the dive shop existed and learned that she was an expert. You offered to set her up in business as long as she did all the work and you took a share of the profits."

Cooper frowned. "I gave her an opportunity that she would never have had otherwise."

They went back and forth like this for another five minutes, but it was clear to Austin that, although this lady's way of doing business might seem predatory, none of this had anything to do with the murders.

"The real question," he asked her when Sheriff Derby ran out of questions, "why did Carla disappear? And do you know where she is?"

"Her disappearance is costing me money," Cooper said. She looked straight into the camera, straight at Austin. "And she disappeared because of you and your partner. She figured that if you found her through the church, found her dive shop, the next thing you would do is look into her citizenship. People like Carla live in fear of deportation every day of their lives. Even after they've been enmeshed in the community. She disappeared because she thought she was going to get deported so she may as well hide in another state."

Austin figured this was also why she'd lied about it being Ben's idea to dive at Deception Pass in the first place. She knew that finding that body would bring scrutiny, and she'd instinctively tried to deflect responsibility.

"Do you know where she is?" Derby asked.

Cooper shook her head. "I think she's in California. We've had to cancel a bunch of scheduled dives."

"Three people have been murdered," Kendall said. "A few canceled dives aren't going to concern us much. Do you understand?"

The woman nodded.

"The fastest way to make some headway here is for you to find her and get her on the phone with us," Austin said. "Can you do that?"

"I'll try," Cooper said.

Half an hour later, Austin got a call from Lucy. Kicking his feet up on the table, he answered, "Any luck down at the bridge?"

"Get out to Bainbridge Island," Lucy said. "Local police there got a call. A woman is missing. Marjorie 'Madge' Evering. Seaside Cedars Retirement Community, just a few blocks from the ferry."

Austin swung his feet down from the table and ended the call.

"Kendall," Austin turned to face her.

"I heard," Kendall said, already having thrown on her leather jacket. "Let's go."

CHAPTER TWENTY-EIGHT

SEASIDE CEDARS RETIREMENT Community on Bainbridge Island was one of the nicest facilities Austin had ever seen. Nestled among lush, well-manicured gardens, the main building was a charming blend of modern architecture and classic design. Large windows offered breathtaking views of the surrounding forests and the sparkling waters of Puget Sound. The community boasted numerous amenities, including a state-of-the-art fitness center, an indoor swimming pool, and a serene spa. Walking paths meandered through vibrant flower beds and over quaint wooden bridges, creating a peaceful, almost resort-like atmosphere.

Inside, the common areas were just as impressive. High ceilings and ample natural light gave the spaces a warm and inviting feel. Tastefully decorated lounges with comfortable seating invited residents to relax and socialize. Every detail, from the artwork on the walls to the quality of the furnishings, spoke of luxury and comfort. It was a place designed to provide not just a home, but a vibrant, fulfilling lifestyle for its residents.

On the drive over, Austin had connected with the office

manager, a young woman named Olivia, who assured them she would have all senior management available when they arrived.

And Olivia was there to greet them in the lobby. "Detectives Austin and Shaw?"

"Yes," Austin said, shaking her hand.

Her striking red curly hair caught the light streaming through a skylight, giving her an almost fiery aura. "Come with me. I'll find Jessica, *she's* in charge here."

Austin thought she caught a hint of an attitude in her tone. "She a pretty tough boss?"

"Tough, I guess so, she runs this place like a military unit, and she never misses *anything*."

Austin wanted to follow up, but didn't have time as they were greeted by Jessica walking briskly down the hall. Somewhere between thirty and forty years old, she carried herself with a grace that made her seem like she was from a different era.

After brief introductions, Jessica said, "We called you in the minute we heard Madge missed her cruise. This is not like her *at all*. I've never lost a resident before. We just *have* to find her."

"You did the right thing," Austin reassured her, "and we're here now to do just that, find her."

"I'm imagining you'll want to see the video surveillance," Jessica said.

"We will," Kendall said.

"I'm having maintenance personnel pull the tapes from this morning," Jessica said authoritatively. "They should be sending us the video clips any minute."

"Good." Austin was eager to look at these.

Tall and slender, Jessica's sable hair was neatly pinned up, revealing delicate features and a composed demeanor. Her eyes had a ring of gold around the pupil that faded into a striking shade of green and conveyed both a sharp intelligence and, the way they darted from staff member to resident to Austin to a subtle stain on the carpet, made Austin think there wasn't a single detail she would leave unnoticed.

Leaving Olivia behind, Jessica led them back to her office, where she sat down, crossed her legs, and set her hands on the table. "The resident's full name is Marjorie Evering. Everyone here calls her Madge. She was on her way to a cruise, and we ordered her a car service as usual. That was this morning around 9 AM. We got a call from the friends who were supposed to meet her on the cruise ship. She never showed up. Then we called local police."

"And they called us because we're already working on multiple cases of missing elderly folks," Kendall said.

Austin noticed that she didn't say "deceased," likely so she wouldn't set Jessica off into a panic. The truth was, Austin had no idea whether this disappearance was even connected to their victims, but it was as good a lead as they had right now.

"We will need the name of the car service," Austin said.

Jessica slid a piece of paper across the desk. "All the information is there. They have a rotating crew of drivers. I called myself, and they said that one of their newer drivers did the call this morning. Of course, they tried her cell phone and a home line she had listed and received no answer. We have no idea what this is. They could be dead in a ditch somewhere after having been through a car accident or..." She trailed off.

Austin tried to add a note of comfort in his voice, but he had a hunch he wanted to pursue and he had to come right out with it. "Like Detective Shaw said, we've been investigating a series of crimes against the elderly. I don't suppose you have any information on a man named Jack Ulner."

"The name rings a bell," Jessica said.

Standing, she walked to a filing cabinet behind her desk and began flipping through some papers with careful precision. "Here he is," she said. "He lived here from 2020 to 2022. Transferred to a small place in Poulsbo, according to the file." She showed Austin a picture and it was the same Jack Ulner they'd met at the small facility in Poulsbo, the man whose shoe had ended up on their John Doe, then in the waters beneath Deception Pass Bridge.

"Why did he leave here?" Austin asked.

"I wasn't hired until last year, so I don't know him personally, but..." Jessica continued speaking, but now in a hushed tone, "usually people only leave here one of two ways, feet first or with empty pockets. Unfortunately, it's usually both. Madge, however, she's so healthy and wealthy, I don't expect she'll ever have to leave." Jessica almost smiled, but then a sober look took over her face. "If we find her, and bring her home, that is."

Austin held up a hand, his mind racing. "Your employees here," he said, "has anyone been acting strange lately? Any new hires or employees who have left suddenly?"

"I would have to check in with our HR director, Sandra, to provide you with details of that kind. We are always hiring new people for the kitchen and the grounds. It's hard to keep anyone on the job these days. Our core staff has been fairly stable, but we also have some volunteers."

"Do you have photos of your employees and volunteers?" Kendall asked.

"We do," Jessica said. "We keep digital copies of the photos that we print out on everyone's name badge. Follow me." She stood up and led them through the hallways of the facility back to a lounge area that had a door off to the right. "Wait here for a moment and I will check." She disappeared behind the door.

Austin said to Kendall, "I bet everything I hold dear

that someone involved in this case works here." He paced anxiously, waiting for Jessica to return.

"I agree," Kendall said. She had stopped by a large wall covered with a printout that read: *Celebrate Our Fabulous Employeess!*

Austin thought the extra 's' was likely a typo and not intentionally placed there for emphasis.

Below the banner was a series of photos with people's names or nicknames written underneath, and when Austin noticed Kendall scanning them, he joined her. Suddenly, Kendall lurched forward and pointed at a photo of a man making a peace sign with his fingers in the bottom right corner of the page.

Austin recognized him. "Isn't that, what's his name?"

"Damn right it is. Jacoby."

"Oh, damn," Austin muttered. "Damn damn *damn*!" It was the man who'd volunteered to have his neighbor, Forest, have his aunt's social security checks sent to his trailer. The man they'd let go.

Austin led Kendall into the room without bothering to knock. There, he found Jessica and Sandra the HR Director trying to pull up the files of photographs of the employees. Neither seemed to know how to work their own system.

"Jessica," Austin said, his voice hard and demanding. "You have an employee here named Terrence Jacoby?"

Sandra, a slender Filipino woman, stood up. "Sure. TJ. He called in sick today. Covid, he thought. He sounded pretty bad so we sent him to get a test. We still have pretty strict protocols around Covid here, what a nightmare. All of the women just love TJ. And he never misses leading the reading club meetings. That reminds me, I need to get someone to cover for him, those readers get very upset when the plot goes off course."

"How long has he been working here?" Austin asked.

"He's a staple here, isn't he?" Jessica directed her question to Sandra.

"He's been working here for years," Sandra agreed.

The computer dinged. "Are those the employee photos?" Austin asked. "Don't think we'll need those anymore."

"No," Sandra said, sitting at her computer, "that's the surveillance video. Maintenance sent it over."

They huddled around her computer and watched as the video played. There was Madge, a woman who seemed to be living about twenty years younger than her age, heading out the front door and getting into a black sedan. The driver had managed to keep her or his back to the camera while putting Madge's bags in the trunk, and seemed to do so on purpose.

Austin pulled out his phone and quickly texted the plates to Samantha back at the office, keeping one eye locked on the screen.

"Stop the video," Kendall instructed.

Sandra pressed the space-bar on her keyboard and the video paused on the face of the brunette that was driving Madge Evering, a side angle caught through the window as she pulled out of the parking lot.

"We know this woman, Austin," Kendall said.

"We do," Austin said. He turned to Jessica. "Do *you* know this woman? And, if so, can you tell us how she might be connected to TJ?"

"I've never seen her before," Jessica said.

"Same," Sandra agreed.

"The woman's name is Christine," Austin said. "She runs a little adult family home in Poulsbo. Does that help you to recognize her? Would TJ also work for another company caring for people?"

"Like I said, I've never seen the woman before," Jessica said. "And TJ picks up every extra shift we have to give him.

I don't see how he would find the time to work anywhere else. He probably brings in something comparable to my salary with the amount of overtime he chooses to take. It's no wonder he's home sick today. He works too many hours for us, if you ask me."

Sandra was leaning in and taking a closer look at the still frame. "You said her name was Christine?"

"Yes," Kendall said.

"Christine is a pretty common name. But all the old ladies here are jealous, or at least pretend to be jealous, of TJ's girlfriend. I hear that her name is also Christine. I've never met her, but from the surveillance footage, she looks like she might be TJ's type."

"How so?" Jessica asked.

"Well, you know how he's always facetiously flirting with the white haired women around here?" Sandra continued. "He always cuts things off by telling them he shouldn't have gotten them all riled up because, in truth, he prefers brunettes."

Austin's mind was going a mile a minute. The woman driving the vehicle definitely looked like Christine from the adult family home. But Austin was sure there was still something he was missing.

He couldn't be in two places at once, but he knew someone needed to search TJ's home and someone needed to visit the adult family home where Christine worked and lived. Likely, the two of them were in this together. Austin thought of Hank Butterfield, Helen Virginia Fullman, and their John Doe drowning victim. His gut told him there was a financial aspect to this whole case. And now Madge Evering, who, according to Jessica, was rich.

He felt it highly probable that TJ, Christine, and possibly even TJ's neighbor Forest had been working together to swindle the seniors of their community for some time.

"Jessica, please send over everything you have in his file," Kendall said. "Any screenings you did, his hiring date, absolutely everything. Any special connections he had with residents. *Anything*." She pulled out a card and handed it to her. "Email it to me there, urgently."

Without another word, Austin hurried out, ripping the photograph of TJ off the wall from the *Employeess* roster on his way to the door.

Kendall was close on his heels.

CHAPTER TWENTY-NINE

FIFTEEN MINUTES LATER, they were crossing over the bridge, leaving Bainbridge Island, passing the Suquamish Casino on their left, and entering Poulsbo.

They had called Jimmy and Lucy, who were going to head for the adult family home on Big Valley Road while Austin and Kendall, who were at least twenty minutes behind, would try to secure a search warrant for TJ's home on the drive to meet them.

They had already sent officers to his residence, who had confirmed that there didn't seem to be anyone home and were waiting at the ready to execute the warrant once it was served.

Austin had tried three different judges and none was willing to provide a warrant without much more information, in writing. One judge even told him, "The last guy you brought in, Ben Davis, is currently filing charges against your department for malicious prosecution as well as a fourth amendment claim so no, Mr. Austin, I won't give you a search warrant."

They still hadn't received any word from Jessica either, though Austin knew it would take them some time to get the files together, especially given that they didn't seem to understand their own computer system.

Samantha had been much quicker to find more on Madge Evering. As they drove, Austin listened intently to Samantha's voice coming through the car phone. She had managed to dig up the octogenarian's financial records. "Austin, this lady is what we young people are calling 'stupid rich,'" Samantha began. "She has multiple millions of dollars spread across savings, checking, and investment accounts. We're talking about major wealth here. Her checking account *alone* has a balance that would be a comfortable retirement fund for most people. She has significant investments in blue-chip stocks, bonds, and a diverse portfolio that's been well-managed. There are also several real estate holdings in her name, including a few rental properties that bring in a steady income. Her net worth is well into the tens-of-millions range."

"And she's staying at the fanciest retirement community on Bainbridge Island," Austin added.

"With that kind of money, this could be a ransom situation," Kendall said.

Austin was thinking the same. "All three of the other victims were fairly poor and didn't have many friends or family. They were, in many respects, the most vulnerable among us. Madge is the opposite. Very well off financially, well-known in the community and in her retirement home."

"She's the exact opposite of the other victims," Kendall agreed. "Samantha, who are the beneficiaries of her will, her estate, if she dies?"

"Hold on," Samantha said. After a moment, she was back on the line. "Don't have any solid information on that, but in the paperwork we were able to get, her will was still the same one she'd set up with her husband over a decade earlier."

"See if you can find anything else," Austin said before ending the call.

"I'll call Jimmy and give him at ETA," Kendall said.

CHAPTER THIRTY

"THEY'RE ABOUT FIFTEEN MINUTES AWAY," Jimmy said, ending the call.

Lucy was doing sixty miles an hour down Big Valley Road and hit the brakes hard before taking a sharp left into the long driveway. "They must be burning rubber to get here, too. We can check this out without them," she said. "They were here the other day, and I don't think it is a high level of danger."

She pulled to a stop next to a brown pickup truck and hopped out, Jimmy right on her tail. At the top of the steps, they knocked on the door.

There was no answer.

Jimmy had wandered down the porch and was peeking through some windows. "The lights are on, and I hear faint music. People are definitely in there."

Lucy knocked again, louder this time. She waited a few seconds and then turned the knob on the front door. "It's unlocked."

Lucy drew her firearm, and Jimmy did the same, both moving with practiced precision. They cleared the entryway, their steps silent and measured. The house was eerily quiet, save for the faint hum of distant music.

In the small kitchen, the counters were clear, and the wide porcelain sink was empty. They moved on, checking three first-floor rooms. Each door was locked, and no sounds came from within.

They ascended the stairs, Lucy leading, Jimmy right on her shoulder. Two more locked doors greeted them on the second floor.

Finally, they reached a narrow stairway leading up to the attic. Lucy paused, hearing the creak of floorboards above. She exchanged a glance with Jimmy, who gave a nod when she pointed upward.

Carefully, they climbed the steps, each one protesting with a muffled creak under their weight. The sounds from above grew louder, more distinct. Something or someone was up there.

Lucy tightened her grip on her firearm, every sense on high alert, ready for whatever awaited them in the attic.

Madge didn't know where she was, and she had no idea how she'd ended up tied to a wheelchair in this basement. And what was that smell? Coming to, her confusion and fear turned to a horror she had never known before. She'd been drugged and kidnapped.

TJ was there, the friendly aide who'd often given her a little extra champagne. And who was that woman? Yes, that was her. The driver who had picked her up that morning. But what were they doing? And where were they?

In front of her, a staircase seemed to lead up to the first floor of whatever building she was in. To her right was a door that led into another section of the basement. And to her left, TJ and the driver had been coming and going, carrying a few boxes and bags out another door that seemed to lead up some steps to the outside; it let in a little sunlight each time they opened it.

She tried to twist her wrists against the duct tape, but it was no use. Despite the water aerobics classes that she took three times a week, she wasn't strong enough to break through that duct tape.

But what did they want with her?

And, good Lord, what was that terrible smell?

"Kitsap County Police, open up!" Lucy yelled, banging on the attic door. There was no answer, but again she heard the floorboards creak.

"I can bust through this door with a single kick," Jimmy whispered. "Should I?"

Lucy nodded. "See, it's not so difficult to check in with me before demolition ensues."

"Lucy-o-melodrama," Jimmy said as he moved in front of her toward the door. "Demolition and construction are not the same thing."

Holding onto the railing with one hand, Jimmy leaned back, then brought his leg up and came down with a violent kick just to the right of the door handle. The door cracked and burst open. "And having your mother with us *could be* a wonderful thing," he said as he and Lucy rushed through the doorway in well-practiced synchronization.

They entered the room standing back to back, firearms at the ready.

Lucy's breath caught in her throat when an older woman sat bolt upright in the bed at the center of the room. She wore a quilted maxi-nightgown and was looking confused.

"Kitsap County Police," Lucy barked. "Is anyone else in the room?"

"I don't know where Christine is," the woman said. "I just don't know where she is."

"The room is clear," Jimmy said. "No other doors."

Lucy confirmed this with a quick glance around the room. "Is there anyone else in this house?"

"Of course," the woman said, her voice sweet and somewhat confused. "Lots of them. There always are."

"What's your name, ma'am?" Jimmy asked.

"Crystal," she said, then appeared to think for a while. "Crystal Jackson."

"Are you a resident here?" Lucy asked.

"Of course not. I'm the owner," the woman said. "My daughter Christine runs the day-to-day now." She stood up from the bed slowly and looked down at her pastel pink yellow and orange nightwear, chuckling to herself. "I guess I'm just getting older too, aren't I?"

Lucy was a bit confused by the woman. Crystal looked to be in her mid-sixties or early seventies, but was moving and acting, and *dressing* like she was in her nineties.

"Do you know if Miss Sampson got her medications today?" Crystal asked. "Christine is always forgetting the medications."

"Here's what's going to happen—" Lucy began.

But Jimmy cut her off. "Hi Crystal. It's nice to meet you. Are you able to take us downstairs and show us where everyone is?"

"Yes. We better go down and see if Miss Sampson got her medications. And what about Jack? Did he get his meds? You know he needs his blood pressure medication." She gave a tired laugh. "Don't want him to suffer a stroke on our watch."

Lucy figured that she must have been talking about

people who *used* to live there. It was clear her memory was off somehow, and she seemed genuinely confused or else was an excellent actor.

Jimmy offered Crystal his arm and, like the perfect son, gently led her toward the staircase. Turning over his shoulder, he looked back at Lucy and gave her a wink and a smile. She smiled back with a smirk. He was the paragon of male progeny.

Jimmy turned back to address Crystal. "Take us to where the people are," he said, and they began down the stairs.

CHAPTER THIRTY-ONE

THE SMELL WAS GETTING WORSE.

Madge's hearing had never been the best, and somehow her earpiece had disappeared while she'd been out like a light in the Lincoln. The thing was usually quite secure, so she figured her captors had taken it out. But even without her hearing aid, she could still hear the notes of concern in their voices.

They had stopped hurrying back and forth with boxes and were now huddled together a few feet from her, chatting urgently about something.

Madge only wished that her sense of smell had left her, rather than her sense of hearing. The stench was nearly unbearable. A couple times, TJ had opened the door to the other area of the basement. From her angle, Madge could not see in, but she could smell whatever was back there. Urine and feces and rotting garbage and the dank, dusty, moldy smell so common in basements. All of them were mixed into one stomach-churning odor.

TJ pointed at the ceiling, indicating something above them. Then the woman held her phone up to him. Madge couldn't see the screen, but the way they were staring at it made her think that they didn't like what they saw. Suddenly, TJ hurried over to Madge and wheeled the chair toward the doorway that led up the stairs to the back side of the building.

Now that she was close to both of them, she could hear them speaking.

"Lock the others in," TJ said.

The woman said, "Give me the keys. *You* have the keys."

Flustered, TJ fumbled in his pockets and handed the woman some keys. The woman kept glancing at the stairwell that led down from the first floor. It gave Madge the idea that someone was in the house. Someone they had heard. Perhaps they even had video cameras that appeared on their phones. She had seen that on an episode of Law & Order.

In any case, they were concerned, and that made her more worried for herself. *Shoot the hostage!* That was what one of the terrorists had said in a film she'd watched recently. When the police were closing in, the only thing to do was to shoot the hostage. Didn't want to leave any witnesses.

But they didn't shoot her. As the woman locked the door to the stench-filled area, TJ pulled her wheelchair up the six stairs and out of the basement where they landed in the backyard. Although she was able to see and hear some, she had barely the strength to hold herself upright in the chair. Whatever poison they had given her was still preventing her from using her body at full function.

In the grass, a white van was parked only a few feet from the door. TJ rolled her right up to it, then transferred her through the large opening on the side in a gentle stand-and-pivot maneuver before pushing her upper body hard. This sent her into an uncontrolled roll and landed her feet inside of the vehicle and her face flush against the cold metal floor in the back of the van, which had only one seat next to a small square window.

TJ closed the door in a hurry, leaving the empty wheelchair behind. He disappeared and only a moment later reappeared, hopping into the driver's seat with the woman joining him in the passenger seat. Apparently, they had done whatever they came to do.

As TJ slowly pulled out from around the house, Madge saw that the boxes and papers they had grabbed were scattered in the back of the van's cargo area.

Just like her.

∼

Austin took a sharp right turn down 305 and, a few minutes later, turned onto Big Valley Road.

"What could we have missed at this place before?" Kendall asked after a long silence.

"I don't know," Austin said. "I just don't know."

He'd been thinking back to their visit there and how he'd been slightly distracted by the conversation with Sy that he had in the car right before walking in. Kendall had mentioned them having the most polite babies ever, and Austin now wondered whether that slight distraction had made him miss something about Christine or Jack Ulner.

"I don't understand," Kendall said. "Let's say that Madge's disappearance is directly connected to TJ and the three deaths we know about. The MO doesn't connect."

"My hunch is that this could be an escalation of some sort. Assuming this connects to Forest and the social security check fraud thing, and we all were hoodwinked and he and TJ did have something to do with his aunt's death, Madge's disappearance is upping the game. I don't know how they think they can get her money, but that's gotta be what they are after."

Lucy held her shirt over her nose, which didn't help in the slightest. She knew the smell of death, and that was part of what she was sensing but, there was some much worse odor that was coming from the left side of the basement.

"Where is everybody?" Crystal asked.

The room where they stood was a standard basement space with an epoxy sealant flooring that was made to look like a seashore. Jimmy, Lucy, and Crystal walked a few steps from the bottom of the staircase where they stood on the "sand" to the part where the "ocean" began towards the center of the room.

To the left, there was a wall that looked like it had been recently constructed. Lucy thought she heard a faint noise from the space behind that wall. To their right was a closed door that seemed to lead up some steps to the backyard.

"Yes, where are the people who need their medicine Crystal?" Jimmy asked.

"Oh, that's right. Christine and that terrible TJ did some remodeling around here. This must be the way to their rooms," Crystal said, pointing to the door on the interior wall to the left. "Now where are those keys?" She began to feel around in the pockets of her garment.

"What's out back?" Jimmy asked.

Crystal looked at the door on the exterior wall, a little confused. "Oh, just weeds I'm sure. Now, don't you judge me if you go out there. I'm not much of a gardener. Oh, I bet it's up here."

Lucy went to the exterior door and tried the handle. It was locked. When she turned back toward Jimmy, she saw

Crystal retrieve the key from the top of the door jam and slide it easily into the doorknob, gently pushing open the door.

Lucy couldn't see into the room from where she was, but she heard shuffling and moaning coming from that direction, sounds that hit her like a punch to the gut along with a fresh waft of the terrible, terrible smell.

Standing in the doorway, Crystal let out a gut wrenching scream before passing out, falling into Jimmy's arms.

"Lucy, get in here!" Jimmy called out, his tone urgent.

Just then, Lucy heard the door at the top of the stairs slam shut, and the triangle of light that had illuminated the basement disappeared, leaving them in total darkness. What sounded like locks engaging followed the door slam.

"It's okay, we're here to help," Jimmy's voice cooed softly in answer to the shuffling and moaning.

Lucy thought he must be making his way into the room, though she couldn't see him. "Jimmy, hold on!"

The muffled sound of an engine roaring to life came from the direction of the exterior door. "Jimmy, I hear them out back, they've locked us in down here. I'm going to find us a light switch."

Without the venting via the upstairs door, the stench was growing worse and worse.

Lucy felt her way along the wall until she reached the door to the room that led to Jimmy and Crystal and what smelled and sounded like something worse than she wanted to imagine.

"Found one," Jimmy said solemnly.

Lucy had never heard his voice sound like that before. They'd been through sad and terrifying experiences together. They'd gone to funerals when people they'd loved died in tragic ways. But Jimmy always held space for people in their grief with humor and grace. Now, what Lucy thought she heard in his voice was complete despair, like he had no hope left at all.

She heard footsteps from above. Must be Kendall and Austin, she thought.

"Okay everyone," Jimmy said in a soft voice. "I'm turning on what I think are the lights."

At the flip of the switch Lucy felt and heard a large oscillating fan spin into motion from the corner. Not a moment later, stark fluorescent track lighting flickered.

With each strobe of illumination, the darkness before them came to horrifying light.

"Dear God," Lucy muttered. "Dear God, no."

CHAPTER THIRTY-TWO

AUSTIN AND KENDALL burst through the front door, guns drawn. The house was eerily quiet, Austin noticed, save for the faint hum of music playing somewhere inside. The air was thick with the stench of something foul, not even the ocean scented air freshener that was still sending up its smoke signal could mask it. The smell made the hair on Austin's neck stand on end.

Kendall retched. She brought her forearm up, smushing the sleeve of her leather jacket against her nose to try to block the smell.

"They should be here," Austin said, glancing at his phone, the screen showing Lucy's last known location. "The tracker has Lucy right where we're standing."

Kendall nodded, her eyes scanning the entryway. "There must be a basement or a hidden room."

Austin followed the sound of the music, which led them into the kitchen. His heart pounded in his chest, a mix of fear and adrenaline coursing through him. The music was louder here, coming from a small radio on the counter. He reached over and switched it off, plunging the house into an even darker silence.

"Let's check the rest of the house," Kendall suggested.

They moved cautiously, clearing room after room. The living room was empty. They found a small dining room and a couple of locked bedrooms upstairs, but no sign of Lucy or Jimmy. And no one answered any of their calls.

The foul odor was less intense as they moved away from the ground floor, but the tension in the air remained steadily palpable.

"Nothing," Austin said, frustration evident in his voice. "We're missing something."

They returned to the kitchen, where the odor had been the strongest, their sense of urgency mounting. Then they found a door they hadn't noticed before. It was built into the wall seamlessly and Austin hadn't noticed it their first time through.

Austin heard a shout coming from below. "Was that Lucy?"

Kendall banged on the door, which was locked.

"Austin, Kendall is that you?" It was Lucy's muffled voice coming through the wall-shaped door, followed by rapid pounding.

Kendall pounded back. "Lucy, we're here."

"Christine and TJ," Lucy yelled. "They got away. We're locked in the basement. It's clear here, but..."

She trailed off, her voice weak.

Austin stepped back, preparing to kick in the door.

"Don't you have a lock pick set?" Kendall muttered. Then she turned back to yell through the locked door. "Lucy, move away from the door. Down the stairs. We're gonna break you out."

Austin had given his to an FBI agent friend, Claire Anderson. "I guess I should get another one."

He busted through the wall-shaped door easily, and the condensed smell that was released in the backdraft hit him like a moist brick wall. He and Kendall descended the stairs into semi-darkness and met Lucy. Her face was ashen and, without a word, she led them into a brightly-lit room.

What Austin saw next was the most horrifying thing he had ever seen.

CHAPTER THIRTY-THREE

THE STENCH WAS UNBEARABLE. The acrid smell of fresh urine and urine turned to ammonia, sweat, bile, feces, and something else Austin couldn't quite place... something that smelled of battlefield, of death itself.

He hoped it wasn't rotting flesh, but feared it was.

He dropped to his knees, gagging while still in the doorway.

The light shining from the ceiling was as overpowering as the smell and, as Austin stood, he saw the horror that had created the smell.

The room held six people tied to mattresses on the ground and gagged, their eyes were wide with fear and desperation, their skin pale and bruised. All were in various states of distress. Their wrists were bound with rough, makeshift ropes that had cut into their flesh, leaving raw, angry, and in some places bloody marks. Some had duct tape over their mouths, while others had cloth gags that had been tied so tightly they left indentations on their cheeks.

The room itself was a hellish tableau of squalor. The floor was covered in grime, and there were makeshift beds —little more than dirty mattresses on the ground—scattered around. Dozens of small opened boxes of baking soda were strung up and left hanging from the ceiling, more thickly set near the door that led to the exit, presumably to mask the smell from getting to the stairs and up to the entry level of the home. Austin remembered he hadn't sensed any foul odor when he'd first arrived to meet with Jack Ulner and Christine.

The baking soda box shadows danced across the walls, which were damp and moldy. In one corner, a large, blue bucket served as a toilet; the stench emanating from it made Austin's stomach churn.

Lucy and Jimmy were working frantically to free the victims, Lucy's face set with determination, her hands shaking as she fumbled with the knots. Jimmy, his usually calm demeanor now a mask of fury, was using his teeth to loosen the ropes around an elderly man's wrists.

Austin and Kendall joined in, working desperately as they moved from bed to bed. The air was thick and warm and moist, the sight before him like something out of a nightmare. As he walked from bed to bed, it was as though wading through a swimming pool of death and disease.

One woman—frail and gaunt—lay motionless on a mattress, her breathing shallow. Her eyes flickered open as Austin approached, and the terror in her gaze was palpable. Another man, with deep-set eyes and skin stretched tight over his bones, struggled weakly against his bonds, his muffled cries of distress sending chills down Austin's spine.

Austin moved quickly, working to free the man.

"Lucy and Jimmy," he said. "Are you injured?"

"No," Jimmy said. "But these people... we need to get them out of here."

Lucy was already helping an elderly woman to her feet. "We need medics, now."

Austin nodded, pulling out his phone to call for backup. There was no service in the basement, so he darted back up the stairs and through the door he'd busted only a few minutes earlier. Out on the front porch, he made the call. "This is Detective Austin. We need immediate medical assistance at our location on Big Valley Road. Multiple victims, severely malnourished and restrained."

After ending the call, he hurried down to help free the final victims from their restraints. His hands shook as he worked, the reality of what they had stumbled upon sinking in.

One man, his face hollow and desperate, clutched at Austin's sleeve, his eyes pleading. "Please," he whispered, his voice barely audible even after removing the gag. "Help us."

Austin started to untie the man's wrists. "We're getting you out of here," he said, trying to keep his voice steady.

He moved to another woman, her eyes vacant and unseeing. She muttered to herself, rocking back and forth as if in a trance. Austin untied her gently, his movements careful. "You're safe now," he murmured, though he wasn't sure if she could hear him.

Every new detail fueled his rage. This wasn't just a crime; it was an atrocity.

The sound of sirens grew closer. Medics and backup officers would be there soon, but for now, they needed to get these people out of here.

They moved quickly, guiding the frail and frightened victims up the stairs and out into the fresh air. The medics arrived just as they reached the front door with the last victim.

Standing on the porch, Austin stepped back and leaned against a window, his body trembling with exhaustion and anger. He watched as the medics tended to the victims, his mind still reeling from the horror they had uncovered.

Kendall came up beside him, placing a hand on his shoulder. "We got them out. We did... we did okay." She sounded like she was trying to convince herself of something. "Every law enforcement agency in the state is looking for Christine and TJ. I... I..." Her voice cracked and she trailed off.

"We were *here!*" Austin shouted. "Right here a few days ago." He kicked an old wooden rocking chair as hard as he could. "How did we miss this? How the hell did we miss this?"

"We need to pick ourselves up," Kendall said.

Austin looked up. "I know and I agree. It's just..."

"I know," Kendall said. "I know."

Austin had seen some things in his twenty years in the NYPD and quite a few things since he'd been working with the Kitsap Sheriff's Department—first as a consultant, then as a private investigator who sometimes helped on cases, and now as a full-fledged detective. But nothing could have prepared him for this.

He couldn't help but think of his own father, as vulnerable as a baby and thankfully with people to look after him. The thought of that basement cell—those innocent people confined to a dungeon of horror—would be with him for the rest of his life.

Then he tasted something he'd never experienced before.

It was as though every kind of chili pepper on earth had been blended together with steel and compressed into a dense disc, a disc into which he was now biting.

Metallic fire was the only way he could describe it.

It was a feeling well beyond rage. It was as though the

flavor of pure, unadulterated violence and vengeance had landed in him.

He was no longer out to enforce the law.

He was out for revenge.

PART 3

TURNING THE TIDE

CHAPTER THIRTY-FOUR

AN HOUR LATER, as darkness fell over the cracked parking lot and the house, now empty except for crime scene investigators dressed in hazmat suits, Austin sat on the steps. He'd called Andy and asked him to feed Run and bring her home with him, anticipating a very late night.

Inside the house, they'd found three other residents, including Jack Ulner, drugged and locked in their rooms, but still alive. Now Jimmy and a team of crime scene specialists were going over every inch of the place. In an ambulance to their left, Crystal, the legal owner of the property, was being examined by an EMT, a requirement before they could interview her.

Photos of TJ were already circulating with law enforcement throughout the state. Marjorie Evering was a missing person now, and her photo was circulating as well. To Austin, the number one priority now was to figure out where they might be going and what they planned to do with Madge.

He stood suddenly when he saw a familiar car approaching. "What the hell is *he* doing here?"

Kendall stood as well. "Oh God," she said. "As though this couldn't get any worse."

County Commissioner Larsen was getting out of the car and walking purposefully toward the crime scene. Behind him were two reporters Austin recognized from the press conference in front of the sheriff's Office.

Larsen stopped abruptly in front of an ambulance, outside of which multiple victims in their seventies and eighties were still being treated for dehydration and malnutrition. Soon they would be taken to the hospital, but paramedics were trying to stabilize them before the trip. One of the reporters pulled out an iPhone and began filming, the other shone a small light on Larsen, who apparently intended to use this misery for a photo op.

Austin began walking slowly toward them, hit first by a wave of disbelief, then rage, as he heard what Larsen was saying.

"I'm standing outside of a group home in Poulsbo, Washington, the scene of a despicable crime and further evidence of the failure of your Kitsap Sheriff's Department. While they've been traipsing around Island County and twiddling their thumbs, under their very noses, a horror show was unfolding."

Austin had had it with this guy.

Bounding across the parking lot, he stood between Larsen and the videographer.

"That's enough," Austin said.

"We have a right to film here," Larsen protested.

"No, you don't," Austin said. "This is a crime scene."

He took Larsen by the elbow and pulled him down the driveway to the edge of the road. "You have a right to film *here*," he said firmly, pointing at the ground. "Cross one inch onto the property again and you'll be put in the back of a squad car."

He had about five inches on Larsen and looked down at him, eyes blazing. Larsen stared back, a slight smile forming on his lips.

"You're the boss, Detective Austin," he said. "At least for now."

As Austin walked back to join Kendall at the car, he noticed that the entire episode had been filmed by Larsen's lackeys in the press.

"I'm glad you did that," Kendall said. "Because I was about to. And I might not have been so polite."

Austin shook his head. There was nothing he could do about Larsen using every crime, every tragedy for his own personal political aims. But he could keep him from doing it within earshot of the victims.

"He's not wrong though," Kendall said. "Not exactly. This is bad. We were at this house a few days ago and we missed it."

Austin felt it like a punch in the stomach. It was true, and he knew it. Not only that, but who knew how long those people had been in the basement?

Likely months. Maybe years.

Austin watched a paramedic attach an IV bag to a little metal frame on a stretcher, then help to hoist an elderly woman into the back of an ambulance. The ambulance pulled away, lights flashing, and turned onto the main road.

Austin pointed toward another ambulance, where Crystal was being released by a paramedic. "We're going to start with her."

Sitting on the steps, Austin took a deep breath and put his hands in his lap, trying to remain calm. "Crystal," he said, "how are you feeling?"

"I feel just fine. I..." She trailed off, shaking her head. She seemed confused, but not unaware of what had been found in her home, in her business.

"Crystal, I'm going to start with a tough question. Did you know there were people locked in the basement?"

Crystal's hair was thin, her eyes shifty, her face bony and gaunt, and her flesh almost gray. She looked as though she hadn't been outside in years and was suffering from physical ailments along with mental ones. Jimmy had mentioned that he and Lucy had found her locked in the attic. Austin wasn't sure, but he doubted she was fully aware of what was going on under her own roof, which allowed him to temper his rage as he spoke with her.

"Sort of," she said uncertainly. "Christine told me they were building more space down there for our residents. She was going to take care of everything."

"Christine, is married to or dating TJ, correct?" he asked.

She grimaced. "I never trusted that TJ. This is all his fault."

"And do either of them have any connection with the Seaside Cedars Retirement Community on Bainbridge Island?" Kendall asked.

Crystal said nothing, just let her head fall back to look up at one of the evergreens swaying above them.

"Crystal," Austin said, "look me in the eyes. You're safe with me, and I can help you. But we need to start at the beginning." He waited for her eyes to lock on his. "Stay with me," he said, "lock in right now, this moment. And tell me everything."

CHAPTER THIRTY-FIVE

IT TOOK over an hour and quite a bit of coaxing from Austin, but Crystal did her best to stay focused. Kendall went back and forth between the interview and the team inside the house as piece after piece of horrifying evidence was uncovered.

Because of the severity of the crime, they were able to get a judge out of a dinner party to finally issue an emergency warrant to search TJ's trailer. The team there was calling Kendall with updates as they found things that might be pertinent to the case. In addition to trying to put together a general picture of the scheme, they were looking for any evidence that might lead them to TJ and Christine and, they hoped, Marjorie Evering.

By the time Austin stood up, his back ached from sitting on the small steps for so long as the night turned cold. He hadn't learned anything that would lead to Madge's location—Crystal seemed to be genuinely ignorant of this element of the crime—but the rest of the story had come together in his mind.

Crystal had started the adult group home in 2006 after a

solid career in healthcare. She was a registered nurse and had all the correct paperwork and business licenses. Judging by early photos, it was a fine facility. Not everyone could afford the higher-end senior living apartments full of amenities and gourmet food, so this was a cheaper alternative that still provided a good place to live for adults who needed medical care they couldn't get on their own.

Things started to go bad with the financial crisis of 2008. Christine, Crystal's daughter, lost her house after her adjustable interest rate turned predatory and her first husband took off, leaving her unable to afford their increased payments. Christine split with her husband and moved into a spare room in the group home belonging to Crystal. Not long after that, TJ started coming around.

According to Crystal, TJ was always looking for an angle, and Christine fell under his sway. Christine had her CNA license and was helping around the facility as it expanded. They added two bedrooms in 2012 and were well-known around the community.

Even TJ helped out sometimes, providing some maintenance and yard work. But slowly, as the 2010s came to an end and the 2020s began, Christine and TJ started taking over more and more of the business.

Crystal didn't want to admit it, but Austin figured it was partially because of Crystal's physical and mental health issues. He also wondered whether Christine and TJ might have *caused* some of those issues.

By 2021, Christine was running everything. Crystal stayed in her attic room more and more, then finally stopped leaving the room at all. Sometimes at night, she would hear things downstairs and try to come out, but the door wouldn't open. When asked, Christine always said it was left locked by accident.

What Crystal didn't know was why there were so many

people in the basement, and why bodies were being found under the bridges. From her perspective, TJ was taking over and Christine was under his thumb. When pressed, she had no idea what motivation they could have had for their heinous crimes.

But Kendall provided those answers. In short, Christine and TJ were bleeding these seniors dry, then disposing of them when they died or ran out of money.

Christine and TJ's crimes were as extensive as they were cruel. They started with stealing Social Security checks, forging signatures to cash them. TJ was adept at covering their tracks, ensuring that any complaints were buried under bureaucratic paperwork.

Overbilling was another facet of their scheme. Christine, leveraging her background as a CNA, would inflate medical expenses, charging the "patients" for treatments and services never rendered. From physical therapy sessions with companies that never existed to medications never administered, the bills were meticulously detailed to avoid suspicion. The victims, already stretched thin, were pushed to their financial limits, paying for care they never received.

And these were just their early crimes.

Gaining control of their patient's bank accounts was next, and this required making sure they had complete control of their bodies. Christine and TJ would gain the trust of their residents, sometimes setting them against their families but usually admitting only residents who had no close family. After promising to manage their finances for them responsibly, they would transfer funds into accounts under their control, slowly draining the savings their captives had built over a lifetime. Their so-called residents were left with nothing and, at this point, they could never be allowed to leave.

The men and women in the basement were essentially

financial hostages. Once Christine and TJ gained control of them, they were deprived of adequate food, water, and medical care, but given just enough to keep them alive for as long as possible. It was a cruel balance, maintaining life at the barest minimum so they could continue siphoning their funds.

And once these unfortunate souls died, Christine and TJ had to dispose of them in any way possible. Like dumping them off a bridge.

Kendall also learned that TJ had been working at Seaside Cedars for years. There he had started scoping out the residents, convincing Jack Ulner and two others to transfer to Crystal's facility when funds got low, but before they got too low to leave TJ and Christine with something to steal.

Austin figured that they'd been looking for a golden goose like Madge for years. And when they'd felt the police closing in on them, they had decided to escalate their crimes to a new level.

Instead of preying only on the most vulnerable seniors— those without much money or family to look after them— this time they chose someone rich. They wanted a mark wealthy enough to leave them rich for life, even if it was someone who would be noticed when she went missing.

But that meant that they had plans to drain her of everything, and to do it quickly.

And once they did, Austin knew they would have no reason to keep her alive.

CHAPTER THIRTY-SIX

AFTER BEING DUMPED in the back of the van, Madge had crawled up into the seat and buckled herself in. She didn't know their ultimate destination, but she knew the streets well, and she knew which direction they were headed.

The drive took them through the winding roads of the Kitsap Peninsula, starting in Poulsbo and heading first on the long straight south-southwest stretch of Highway 3 past Silverdale. The late evening cast a serene, dusky glow over the trees lining the highway, which shielded their view of the suburban neighborhoods tucked behind the evergreen canopy.

They continued through Bremerton and hit the junction where Highway 3 and Highway 16 met. To their left, the shipyards and naval base stood silent but imposing, their communication tower lights flickering above the ships, which were just visible against the darkening sky.

Passing through the hairpin at Gorst, they continued south-southeast through Port Orchard. When they passed the large hardware store that abutted the west side of the highway, Madge thought of her late husband. They used to visit a pizza place here that made the most delicious Hawaiian pizza. They would eat pizza and talk about the poor hostages who had starved to death decades earlier in the neighboring town of Olalla at a place that was colloquially called Starvation Heights. They would also give thanks and count their blessings.

Now Madge felt she was in for a similar fate. As much as she loved and adored the late Mr. Ernest Evering and longed to be by his side once again, she had a strong sense of justice and vowed to live long enough to point an accusatory finger at her captors.

The highway was mostly empty at this hour, the dense trees on either side casting long shadows across the asphalt. Eventually, they turned eastward at the edge of Gig Harbor and Madge watched the vertical suspender cables blip by in rapid succession as they drove under the tall, H-shaped structures that held up the main suspension cables supporting the mile-long colossus that was the Tacoma Narrows Bridge.

At the giant lighted American flag, they took the fast lane to merge onto I-5 Northbound and continued on the highway, passing the quiet streets of the city, where the industrial zones and residential areas were bathed in the orange glow of streetlights. They passed by the towering silhouette of the Tacoma Dome and the quiet expanse of the University of Washington Tacoma campus, before the highway shifted in a true northward direction toward Seattle.

As they approached The Emerald City, the familiar sight of the stadiums came into view, with T-Mobile Park and Lumen Field standing tall, throwing their rich blue neon lights against the dark night sky. The city's towering structures loomed ahead, a glittering array of skyscrapers and buildings. The Space Needle was prominently lit up and they drove in its direction after exiting the freeway.

The drive through the downtown area was a stark contrast to the winding roads of Kitsap, the hustle and bustle of Seattle even at this late hour provided a stark reminder of where they were.

Her captors hadn't wanted to risk being seen on the ferry, she figured, so they had driven from Poulsbo all the way to Seattle under the cover of darkness.

As TJ turned toward the waterfront district and Pike Place Market, the woman who'd posed as her driver—a woman she now knew was named Christine—turned around and spoke to Madge for the first time.

"You have one way to stay alive," she said. "Soon we'll be out of America, and you'll be transferring your fortune to us. Don't try to lie. We already know that you're swimming in cash."

CHAPTER THIRTY-SEVEN

Friday

IT WAS a little after midnight when Austin pulled out of the driveway and onto Big Valley Road, intending to return to the office, when a report came over the police radio.

"Attention all units, this is Central Dispatch with an urgent update. At approximately 10:17 PM today, the Kitsap County Health Department, along with every major hospital in the region, experienced a major cybersecurity breach. An anonymous hacker has infiltrated health records databases... *Pause, CLICK...* The ransom note, discovered minutes later states: 'Your health records database has been hijacked. Deposit ten million USD worth of Bitcoin to the address below within twenty-four hours or all records will be permanently deleted'... *Pause, CLICK...* An internal task force has been assembled to collaborate with cybersecurity experts, and the FBI Cyber Crimes Unit will be contacted for additional support... *Pause, CLICK...* All units are advised to remain vigilant and report any suspicious activity related to this breach immediately. Central Dispatch out."

"What is going on?" Austin asked, mind swimming.

"This is bad," Kendall said.

"Very," Austin said. "And it can't be a coincidence. TJ and Christine are up to something even bigger than we thought."

He knew that the healthcare system relied heavily on accurate and up-to-date patient information. Without these records, doctors wouldn't have access to patients' medical histories, which could lead to misdiagnosis and improper treatments. All scheduled surgeries would come to a halt. Medications that could interact negatively might be prescribed, and allergies might be overlooked, resulting in severe, even fatal, reactions.

The chaos could extend to emergency services as well— paramedics arriving at a scene without critical information on a patient's condition or history could make life-threatening mistakes.

This had all happened before. In 2017, the WannaCry ransomware attack had crippled the NHS, the UK's National Health Service, delaying surgeries and treatments, and forcing hospitals to turn patients away simply because they didn't have the resources to care for the people they'd already admitted. The idea of something similar happening in Kitsap County was terrifying.

The elderly and vulnerable, already targets for Christine and TJ's schemes, would be at great risk on a much wider scale. Austin felt the weight of the potential disaster pressing down on him—this wasn't just about catching criminals anymore; it was about preventing a catastrophe that could cost not only Madge's life, but the lives of thousands of others as well.

Kendall had been quiet a long time, then finally asked, "But how could it be anything *other* than coincidence? Thinking back to our interview with TJ, and going on what

Crystal said about her daughter... I don't know. I don't see how Christine or TJ could have had anything to do with this. This sort of ransomware attack requires advanced technical skills. I mean, did TJ strike you as someone with the sophistication to hack anything?"

Austin's mind was jumping from moment to moment over the last few days, trying to figure out how this breach could be connected to Madge, to TJ, and to Christine.

"No," Austin said. "This has to involve someone higher up. Someone with technical expertise and an understanding of the healthcare system. But who?"

Austin's mind went suddenly blank and he smelled campfire.

It was his synesthesia kicking in, and he knew precisely where this memory came from. Once, early in his relationship with Fiona, she'd been away at a conference for prosecutors, and he'd taken the opportunity to go on a camping trip with a friend from the NYPD. They headed to upstate New York, and, on the last night of their trip, Austin had been lying on his back next to the fire and staring up at the biggest, blackest night sky full of the brightest stars he had ever seen.

His mind had gone completely blank then—all the thoughts, cares, and worries of the world were gone for what seemed like hours but was probably only minutes. When he'd come to, he'd realized that he and Fiona were going to get married. And ever since, he'd been yearning for that moment when he'd smell that campfire again, his mind totally blank.

Now, as they merged onto the highway, it was here again.

"Austin, what is it?" He heard Kendall's voice cutting through the strange blankness. Slowly, he pulled onto the shoulder, unable to focus on the road.

"Austin, what is it?"

"The redhead," Austin said. "Olivia. Do you remember what she said when we were at the Seaside Cedars? Do you remember?"

Kendall cocked her head. "Yes. She said something... or it was *how* she said it. She said that Jessica, the executive director, runs the place like a military unit."

"And," Austin added, "that she never misses anything. *Never. Misses. Anything.*"

"So how is it possible," Kendall asked, her voice full of excitement, "that a dumbass like TJ worked there for years, hatching a plan to kidnap a resident, and Jessica *didn't* notice?"

CHAPTER THIRTY-EIGHT

"GIVE HER THE DRUGS," TJ said. "We're almost there."

"Here," Christine said, holding out three white pills to Madge. "Take these. Swallow them." She offered a water bottle with a flexible straw sticking out of it. "The pills won't kill you, you old hag. If we wanted you dead, you'd be dead already."

When Madge refused to take the pills, Christine said, "I can just force you to take them anyway. I'm in the health-care field too, you know."

Madge shook her head. "You may be able to get me to take them. And that's exactly what you will have to do."

"I'll pull over," TJ said. "You shove them down her throat. Do what you have to do, just make her take them."

"I know," Christine said. "Did you not hear what I was just saying?"

She turned back to face him. "You do *not* need to micromanage me, TJ. Do you think I don't know what we are doing here? I just *can't even* deal with you. I'm tired of it."

"Stop being such a bitch," TJ said under his breath.

"Don't you call me that," Christine said. "You know I don't like that word. I don't like that kind of talk."

A week ago, Madge wouldn't have believed TJ capable of any of this. When he spoke about his *brunette maiden*, as he'd affectionately called her, he would beam with pride.

But Madge knew better now—everything about this man was a lie. Theirs wasn't the wonderful relationship he'd made it out to be. Madge and her husband had gotten into their fair share of arguments over the years, of course. But as they'd matured, they didn't allow their little disagreements to fester, and they never turned into anything major.

"*I don't like that kind of talk. I don't like that kind of talk,*" TJ mocked her, making his voice high pitched and whiny in a way that didn't actually sound like Christine in the least.

These two people, she thought, maybe they had once been close, but now they actually loathed each other.

TJ pulled the van into an alley, stopping at a dumpster. He turned off the headlights and everything went dark.

He unlatched his seatbelt and moved toward Christine.

"What are you doing?" Christine asked. "I told you I'd give her the pills." She began opening her door. "I can handle this."

"I'm not so sure you can," TJ said, his voice menacing. "Let's face it, you're tired of me, I'm tired of you—we're both tired of each other—and, between the two of us, I'm going to be the mature adult willing to deal with this impasse our relationship has come to. Come here, I want you to meet someone."

TJ grabbed Christine by the wrist and pushed himself against her until they shared the passenger seat. He shifted against her body again when he opened the door, forcing her to fall to the ground, where she let out a brief sharp scream as she hit the asphalt.

CHAPTER THIRTY-NINE

IT TOOK Austin only a five-minute call to confirm their suspicions.

For the first time in her tenure at Seaside Cedars, Jessica had left work early. In fact, she'd disappeared not long after Kendall and Austin had left. She hadn't been seen or heard from since.

A quick call to Samantha had given them her home address, which they were now speeding toward, crossing the Agate Pass Bridge and heading onto Bainbridge Island.

They'd stopped at the gas station only long enough to grab caffeinated beverages. It was already midnight, and they weren't planning on going to sleep anytime soon.

Lucy and Jimmy were on the scene at the trailer park. Though they were quite sure no one would return to the group home, a couple officers were stationed there as well.

Jessica's apartment was in the quaint neighborhood of Winslow, a charming downtown area known for its cozy cafés, boutique shops, and tree-lined streets. The buildings were a mix of historic homes and modern apartments, all nestled amidst lush greenery that seemed to glow under the soft, golden streetlights. Austin thought it felt like something from a movie.

Parking their car a block away from Jessica's apartment, they tried to keep a low profile as they approached. The air was cool and crisp, filled with the faint scent of saltwater from the nearby marina. They walked quietly along the cobblestone pathway, the sound of their footsteps unnaturally loud in the late-night stillness.

Reaching Jessica's building, they approached her door with a mix of anticipation and caution. Austin knocked firmly, the sound echoing slightly in the silent night. They waited, listening for any signs of movement inside.

Austin motioned for Kendall to take the left side of the door while he positioned himself on the right. They exchanged a brief nod, signaling their readiness. Austin raised his hand and knocked firmly, three sharp raps that echoed in the stillness. "Kitsap County Sheriff's Department. Jessica, we need to speak with you."

They waited a few moments, ears straining for any sound inside. When none came, Austin tried the door handle, finding it locked. "We need to figure out another way in," he said, turning to Kendall.

"Still no lockpick set then?"

He gave her a brief hard stare—Austin's equivalent of rolling his eyes—then moved to search for another entrance.

Just then, an elderly man in a blue silk bathrobe and monogrammed slippers shuffled down the hallway. His nightwear was of fine quality and looked well cared for, but showed its age at the elbows and seams. Austin stopped to allow the man to approach and, as he moved closer, noted that the man's face was lined with curiosity and concern. "Can I help you officers?" he asked, his voice a raspy whisper.

"Yes, sir," Austin replied. "We're looking for Jessica. We need to get into her apartment for a wellness check. Do you know if there's a building superintendent who can let us in?"

"That would be me," the man said.

"Jessica left work early today," Austin said. "No one has heard from her and we're concerned. Can you let us in?"

"Think she was going on a trip," the man said, as he produced a ring of keys from his pocket. "I saw her leaving with a suitcase late this afternoon."

"What time?" Kendall asked.

"Maybe three."

"Thank you," Kendall said, as the man unlocked the door and stepped back to let them enter.

The apartment was small and neat, a single living area with a modest kitchen to one side and a door leading to what was likely a bedroom. The lights were off and the room was filled with shadows, the only illumination coming from the streetlight outside.

"Clear," Kendall said as they moved through the apartment, checking each room, every corner. The bedroom door was ajar, and Austin pushed it open with his foot, gun at the ready. But the room was empty, the bed made up and untouched.

They holstered their weapons, tension dissipating as they realized they were alone. "It's another dead end," Austin said, frustration creeping into his voice.

Madge watched as TJ let himself down from the vehicle and yanked Christine up by the wrist. She tried to pull away and the two struggled between the passenger seat and the door frame. Sensing an opportunity, Madge inched herself toward the door, hoping she might be able to escape while her captors were engaged in their tussle.

Through the window, Madge caught a glimpse of a figure emerging from behind a dumpster.

It was... who *was* that?

A familiar face, barely illuminated by the interior lights of the van, came into focus.

Madge felt a surge of hope coursing through her body. It was the elegant face of Jessica, the executive director of Seaside Cedars. And for half a moment she doubled her efforts to make an escape in her direction. She was going to be saved.

Then a new terror hit her, more intense than anything she'd experienced since being abducted. How did Jessica know to be here? How was it possible that TJ had pulled into a seemingly random alley and Jessica had been standing there, ready to come to her rescue?

It *wasn't* possible.

"Sweetie," TJ said through a clenched jaw as he pulled Christine roughly to her feet. "I'd like you to meet a real woman. Someone who is kind and gentle with me *always*. A person who has never once insinuated that I'm anything less than a great man. See her? See her there? Get a good look."

TJ held Christine, making her watch as Jessica picked up the water bottle and pills from the alley. Jessica opened the sliding door of the van, then leaned in toward Madge.

The day they'd met, when Madge signed the move-in paperwork for Seaside Cedars, Jessica'd had worn the same *nice to meet you* smile that she offered now.

"Hello there, Madge," Jessica said. "It's time for your medicine."

CHAPTER FORTY

BACK AT THE car near Jessica's apartment, Austin leaned against the bumper. He was about to suggest they head back to the office and sleep there in case anything came in overnight when his phone lit up with a text.

"Weird," he said. "A text from Ridley."

"Governor Ridley?" Kendall asked.

"The one and only," Austin said.

"What does he want?"

Austin read the text aloud. "Because of this ransomware attack, I'm now involved. All hands on deck. Conference call at this number in five minutes."

"That can't be good," Kendall said.

Five minutes later, Austin was on the conference call line, listening as many of the most important people in the state joined one by one. Lucy and Jimmy were there. Then Ridley himself joined, his deep voice a welcome sound in the dark night. Then the director of the Kitsap County Health Department, Washington State's health department, the attorney general, and several other members of the state government joined.

"This ransomware attack," Ridley said, "is deadly serious. I don't think I need to explain that to anyone on this line. The FBI is already involved, folks from the Seattle office. Seemed decent enough, but damn. We never *want* them to be involved."

Just then, another caller joined the line, announcing himself as County Commissioner Marty Larsen.

Austin stayed quiet.

"Governor," one of the health commissioners said, "we need to discuss the possibility of paying the ransom. If these health records are deleted, the consequences could be catastrophic."

"I understand the gravity of the situation," Ridley replied. "But paying the ransom could set a dangerous precedent. We can't guarantee the hackers won't just erase the records anyway after receiving the payment."

"Exactly," another commissioner interjected. "We need to find out who is behind this. Someone with inside knowledge of our systems had to have orchestrated this attack."

"Do we have any leads on who it might be?" Ridley asked.

There was a brief pause before one of the health department officials spoke up. "We've been looking into it, but so far, nothing concrete. It could be a disgruntled employee, or it could be someone with outside access. Either way, they're working with sophisticated hackers."

"I think I know who might be behind it," Austin said, breaking his silence.

Larsen's voice boomed through the line. "This can't be left to the bumbling fools of the Kitsap County Sheriff's Department! We need real professionals handling this. In my opinion, we should welcome the help of the FBI."

"Commissioner Larsen," Ridley interrupted, "take a breath. We need—"

"But Mr. Ridley I—" Larsen interrupted.

Ridley interrupted right back. "I think you mean *Governor* Ridley. Now, County Commissioner Larsen, I need you to be silent." Ridley paused. "Austin, go ahead."

Austin took a deep breath. "Her name is Jessica Blackstone and she's the executive director of..."

Austin was distracted by Kendall holding up her phone in front of his face. It seemed to be an urgent bulletin from the Seattle PD.

"Jessica Blackstone," he said again. "Look into her. Executive Director of the Seaside Cedars facility on Bainbridge Island. We believe she is connected to this ransomware attack, we are here at her apartment and she's in the wind."

"Good," Ridley said, "we will get that out there. I've promised the FBI that they can take lead on this, which means, Austin, Lucy, don't do anything without their say so. And please believe me when I tell you, I hate having to make you take a back seat just as much as you hate to be stuck there."

Austin had largely tuned him out as he read the report on Kendall's phone.

URGENT POLICE BULLETIN

Subject: Possible Breakthrough in Ransomware Attack - Immediate Attention Required

From: Seattle Police Department

To: All Law Enforcement Agencies

Incident: Discovery of a Key Witness Related to Ransomware Attack

Details: At approximately 1:30 AM, a woman was found wandering the streets of downtown Seattle, exhibiting multiple injuries, signs of confusion, and possible drug intoxication. The individual had sustained a significant fall and was initially unresponsive to questioning. Upon regaining some clarity, she identified herself as Christine Jackson and claimed to have critical information regarding the ongoing ransomware attack against the Kitsap County hospitals and health systems.

Additional Points:

- She mentioned that a hostage is involved in the situation.
- She stated that she had been double-crossed and drugged.

Current Status: After making these statements, Christine Jackson began ranting and raving before losing consciousness. She has been transported to the hospital for immediate medical attention and is currently under observation.

Priority: This information is deemed critical. All responses should be treated with the utmost urgency.

CHAPTER FORTY-ONE

IT WAS NEARLY 3:00 AM.

Illuminated only by the glow of a street lamp, Austin walked another lap around the car. For the last hour, Kendall had been calling all her contacts in the Seattle Police Department to see if she could find out anything else about the bulletin, or who was running things on their end.

On the call, Austin had agreed to drop the case because that's what Ridley and the other higher-ups had demanded. He had no intention of doing so, but there was no way he was going to win an argument on that particular call, so he decided to go with a tried and true method: ask forgiveness, not permission.

Kendall stopped suddenly right in front of Austin. "What about, what's her name?"

Austin shrugged.

"You know, the FBI woman who you worked with on the thing. Claire something?"

"Anderson."

"What's her role over there?" Kendall asked.

"She's part of a small, specialized task force. She wouldn't be assigned to anything involved in this."

"But she might know who is, or at least be able to get us *something*."

"She's probably sleeping," Austin said.

Kendall squinted at him. "Just call her."

Austin pulled out his phone. After the case they had worked together at Mystery Bay State Park, he had taken her number, though they hadn't spoken much. The call went to voicemail after five rings.

"Try again," Kendall demanded.

Austin did, and Claire picked up after a few rings sounding groggy. "Austin? What the hell time is it?"

"I'm sorry, Claire, it's about three in the morning. I wouldn't call if it wasn't important."

"Hold on," she said. "Let me sit up. What's going on? Is everything okay?"

"I don't know if you saw before you went to bed about the ransomware attack on the health system?"

"I saw it on the news right before I went to bed," Claire said. "But it's not my purview."

"I know," Austin said, "but don't you have a tech expert on your team? Any chance she would like to be involved?"

"CTF has their own people," Claire said. "The Cyber Task Force specializes in investigating cybercrimes, including ransomware attacks. Like it or not, cybercrime is becoming a bigger part of the world and is often tied, as in this case, to real-world crimes involving violence or kidnapping."

"Look," Austin said, "we know this thing ties into a murder investigation we've been conducting over here in Kitsap County."

"I *live* in Kitsap County," Claire reminded him.

Austin had forgotten. He thought of Claire as a Seattle

person because that's where her office was located, but the truth was she lived only fifteen minutes from him in the beachside town of Kingston.

"Can you make a call?" Austin asked. "Call your tech person. What's her name?"

"Violet," Claire said. "But like I said—"

"I wouldn't ask unless it was important. Is there any chance you can provide us some cover, jump into this thing, and let us tag along?"

Claire was silent for a long time. Then he heard the creak of a bed as though she was standing up. "Now that I'm awake... Austin, let me call you back in five minutes. There may be something I can do."

The call ended and Austin again began walking slow laps around the car. The street light above him flickered, and he pulled up the collar of his jacket against the cool wind blowing in from the water.

Claire didn't call back in five minutes and she didn't call back in ten minutes. But when she finally called back after twenty, she'd done more than Austin ever expected.

"Be at the Bainbridge Island Fire Department's helipad in an hour," she said. "You'll be meeting Field Agent Jack Russo. He kind of has a thing for choppers."

The helicopter lifted off from Bainbridge Island, the rotors slicing through the stillness of the early morning. It was just past 4:00 AM, and the world was cloaked in darkness, save for the faintest hint of dawn creeping along the horizon. Austin glanced at Kendall beside him, her face illuminated by the dim glow of the cockpit instruments.

The pilot, a stern-faced man whose name Austin hadn't caught, guided the small FBI chopper smoothly into the air.

Jack Russo, Claire's contact, sat opposite them, his eyes scanning the water below.

As they crossed the Sound, the deep black of the night sky began to give way to a murky blue. The transition from night to dawn was subtle, a gradual lightening that made the water below look like an inky expanse. Austin's heart pounded, a mix of adrenaline and the urgency of their mission. The hum of the rotors filled the cabin, punctuated by occasional radio chatter between the pilot and air traffic control.

"How are you going to justify this?" Austin asked.

Jack turned to him and spoke, but Austin only heard him through the headset. "If the ransomware attack is connected to a serial killing, I can say that I was doing a little proactive work on the murder investigation. After all, it kind of reminds me of a case I worked on in Oregon a couple years back."

"It does?" Kendall asked.

Jack looked at her, stone-faced, but said nothing.

Austin knew what he was implying. He could *say* that it reminded him of a case he'd worked back in Oregon, which meant it could be an interstate case, which meant it was possible to justify getting involved. It was a stretch, but probably not enough of one to get him fired. In any case, Claire had stuck her neck out for them, and Austin wouldn't forget it.

The lights of Seattle appeared in the distance, a cluster of twinkling points that grew larger as they approached. The faint outline of the city skyline was becoming more distinct against the backdrop of the slowly brightening sky. They flew low over the water, the chopper banking slightly as the pilot aimed for their landing spot.

Jack said, "My contact in the Seattle PD says that they've been interrogating Christine. She claims she was once part of the plan but got double-crossed. The meetup was set for 5 AM, though her partner TJ never told her the exact location of the getaway boat. Seattle PD has been searching all of the downtown marinas and staking them out. They've narrowed it down to a few, and my contact believes they will most likely be at one in particular—Emerald Cove Marina."

Austin knew the marina. It was one of the nicer ones in Seattle, populated by larger, faster boats. Plus, it was a bit more secluded compared to the other marinas, making it a perfect spot for a swift getaway.

Jack continued, "They believe the plan is to get the hostage to international waters as quickly as possible. Bitcoin, of course, is a lot tougher to trace than a bag of cash or a bank transfer of U.S. dollars."

As the helicopter descended toward Emerald Cove Marina, the early morning light began to outline the shapes of boats and docks. The rotors whipped the water below into a frothy mist. Austin spotted a sleek speedboat at the far end of the pier. Several figures were hastily boarding, one of them clearly being pushed into the boat, their hands bound. The bound woman moved much more slowly, and Austin figured it had to be Madge.

At Jack's direction, the chopper touched down near Pier 66, close to the marinas and ferry terminal, the thump of the helicopter skids meeting the ground sending a jolt through the cabin.

Austin unbuckled his harness and followed Kendall out into the cool air of dawn.

CHAPTER FORTY-TWO

AUSTIN LED THE WAY, sprinting down the long dock with Jack and Kendall close behind. They reached the end of the dock just as the speedboat disappeared into the darkness of the pre-dawn light.

Austin turned to Jack. "Do you have the authority to commandeer a boat?"

Jack nodded, scanning the marina. "We might not need to. The FBI has a facility nearby."

He pulled out his phone, quickly dialing a number. "This is Agent Jack Russo. We need immediate access to a fast-response boat at Emerald Cove Marina. High-priority pursuit."

While they waited, Jack ran back to the helicopter. When he returned, he said, "He's got enough fuel to pursue them for an hour or two. He can likely get us a visual and a direction."

Within minutes, Austin heard the hum of an engine approaching. An unmarked black boat, sleek and clearly built for speed, glided into view. A fellow agent waved them aboard. "Compliments of the FBI," he said, passing Jack the controls before hopping out.

"All hands on deck!" Jack shouted.

Austin and Kendall jumped aboard and Jack wasted no time, pushing the throttle forward. The boat surged ahead, its powerful engines roaring to life.

"Can you drive this thing?" Jack asked Kendall, preparing to hand over the controls. "I want to see if I can get a visual with my binoculars, and I need to get on with the agent in the chopper."

"I thought you'd never ask," Kendall said. "I came in second in the Pacific Northwest youth Power Boat Championships."

Austin was skeptical. "How long ago was that?"

"Why should that matter?" she asked.

Austin was going to object, but it wasn't like he thought he could do better. "Never mind. Just... be careful, okay? This thing sounds like it can really fly."

"Have your own children if you want to be somebody's father," Kendall said. "I already have a dad."

"Noted," Austin said.

Jack stepped aside and Kendall took the wheel.

The marina faded behind them as they sped out into open water. The early morning light cast a faint glow on the waves, the first hints of dawn beginning to break the darkness. Austin scanned the horizon, but the fleeing speedboat was nowhere in sight.

Jack was on the radio with the pilot. "We need a visual. Can you spot them?"

The pilot's voice crackled over the radio. "Negative. They're not in sight. We're sweeping north."

Austin's eyes darted left and right, trying to catch a glimpse of the boat. Behind them, the Seattle skyline was falling away and the calm water reflected its now distant silhouette. The air was cool, the gentle breeze picking up as they moved farther from the city.

Kendall said, "Jack, get them to cover a wide arc north of our position. We'll maintain our current speed and direction."

Jack relayed their coordinates to the pilot. "Keep us updated on any changes. Over."

Minutes ticked by, feeling like hours. The sound of the boat's engines filled the silence and, for the first time, Austin felt the fatigue start to hit him. He'd been going for twenty-four hours straight.

He could really use one of those caffeinated beverages they'd left back in the car on Bainbridge Island, but his eyes never left the water as he searched for any sign of the speedboat.

"I think I got a visual on them." The pilot's excited voice broke the silence. "Heading north, a few miles south of Whidbey."

Kendall adjusted course slightly and pushed the throttle, increasing the speed. Austin held onto the railing as the boat bounced up off a wave. Though he could still see the water, they were heading into a fog.

The radio crackled. "Visibility is dropping fast up here," the pilot reported. "We've got thick fog rolling in. We'll have to turn back."

"Can you give us a few more minutes?" Jack asked.

"Afraid not. We're already flying blind up here. Instruments are reading near-zero visibility ahead, and we can't risk it. We need to head back to avoid disorientation or a potential collision. You're on your own from here."

The helicopter's hum faded as it turned back toward Seattle, leaving them to continue the pursuit alone.

Five minutes passed, then another five, but they never caught sight of the speedboat.

Kendall glanced at Austin. "What do you think?"

Austin was about to suggest that they circle back around when he spotted a distant shape moving across the water. "There!" Austin pointed. "That's got to be them."

They were approaching the waters near the south end of Whidbey Island and Kendall turned slightly west, following the path of the speedboat and pushing their own vessel to its limits.

"Just stay steady," Jack said. "See where they're going."

Kendall kept a steady pace about a hundred yards behind the fleeing speedboat, maintaining visual contact as it headed north around the west side of Whidbey Island. The early morning sun was now fully up, casting a bright light on the water and illuminating the path ahead.

Kendall adjusted the throttle slightly, ensuring they kept the distance consistent. "My bet is they're heading for one of the little islands," she said.

Jack, now holding a pair of binoculars, continued to observe the speedboat. "They're not trying to lose us, at least not yet. I agree with Kendall. Might be heading for the San Juans."

As they pushed further north, the fog lifted completely and Austin caught a glimpse of Deception Pass Bridge to their right as the coastline of Whidbey Island gradually faded behind them. He leaned against the railing, watching the speedboat intently as they weaved through the small islands and channels, the scenery changing, but their target remaining constant.

Jack grabbed the boat's radio and called the helicopter pilot. "We need you to call in for backup. We think they're heading for the San Juans. Let them know our position. We're closing in."

The pilot's voice crackled back. "Copy that. I'll relay your position and request backup. Stay safe out there."

Kendall kept her focus on the waters ahead. "They might be trying to lose us in the maze of islands."

Jack nodded, binoculars still trained on the speedboat. "Looks like they're slowing down slightly. They could also be running low on fuel."

Jack handed the binoculars to Austin. "See what you think."

Steadying himself as best he could, he tried to get a visual. "Can you get any closer?" he asked Kendall.

She sped up gradually and, as she did, TJ came into focus, and so did the woman next to him. "That's Jessica," he said. "Like we thought. Madge Evering is strapped to a seat."

"How does she look?" Kendall asked.

"Alert, and pretty good despite everything." She looked better than Austin felt, that was for sure.

"They're heading for the shore," Kendall said.

"That's the south end of Decatur Island," Jack offered. "Not a lot there."

Austin moved the binoculars from their boat to the shore they were approaching. "Oh no," he said. "Looks like there's an airstrip and they have a small plane waiting."

CHAPTER FORTY-THREE

AS THEY NEARED THE ISLAND, about a hundred yards from shore, Jack pulled out his cell phone.

Austin looked over Jack's shoulder. "Something that can help us out?"

"Violet from my S.W.O.R.D. team has been working on the ransomware and cyber-attack. She texted. Says the medical records will be difficult to free up—they're already locked, and they're also on a dead man's switch."

"What does that mean?" Kendall yelled over the boat's engines.

Austin gripped the railing tight. "It means the data is set to auto-erase unless manually freed, usually after the ransom is paid. It means we have a better chance of getting the information back if we keep TJ and Jessica alive."

"Yes," Jack continued. "They've set the system to wipe the data permanently."

They were now only about thirty yards behind the speedboat, and Austin watched as they ran their boat into the sand.

Jack tapped out a quick message and sent it. He stowed his phone and pulled out his firearm in one smooth motion.

TJ got out of the boat first, yanking Madge awkwardly behind him, followed by Jessica, who stumbled over the side of the boat and fell onto the sandy beach.

"Stop," Austin yelled over the sound of the engine, but the noise was too loud and they were still too far away to be heard.

Kendall navigated their boat directly up alongside the other and, the moment it stopped, Austin leapt out, gun at the ready, followed by Jack.

At a full sprint, they made their way up the beach, following the path taken by TJ, Jessica, and Madge. Cresting a slight bank, Austin got a visual.

The landing strip was tiny, barely more than a flat stretch of compacted dirt and gravel, just long enough for a small plane to make a hasty departure.

"Stop!" Austin shouted. He was gaining on them easily because Madge was slowing them down, despite being in phenomenal shape for her age.

"We will fire!" Jack called.

The three were five yards from a single-engine Cessna, maybe forty feet long, weathered but well-maintained. It had a white fuselage and faded blue stripes along its sides. It was the kind of reliable aircraft that could make a long trip from the San Juan Islands to Mexico with careful planning and a couple fuel stops. In the cockpit a single pilot was visible through the windshield, his hands adjusting the controls. The propeller spun at full speed, and the plane's engine roared steadily, ready for takeoff.

Austin was gaining on them, and when they were only a few feet from the plane, he brought every ounce of force into his voice that he could muster.

"TJ," he shouted, "I don't want to, but I *will* shoot you.

Turn around with your hands up. Jessica, you too. Let the hostage go."

A yard from the stairs leading into the plane, TJ turned around suddenly, and that's when Austin saw the gun. TJ swung it up quickly, pressing it to the back of Madge's head as he sidestepped behind her, using her as a shield.

Jessica had a gun as well, and she was pointing it straight at Austin.

Jack had somehow fallen behind, but now stood beside Austin and Kendall at the ready.

"TJ, Jessica," Austin said, his hands gripping firmly on his weapon. "There's no way this can end well for you. You *know* that. Backup is on the way. There's no way that plane ends up where you want it to. Don't do this. You don't have to do this."

He saw the fear in TJ's eyes. His hand was shaking.

"Let Madge go," Austin said. "Just let her walk away. That's the best thing you can do for yourself right now."

"And for your *baby*," Jack said.

Austin glanced at him out of the corner of his eye. Was he bluffing or... no. He wasn't bluffing. Austin knew of Violet Wei's reputation and, if Jack had asked for info on the couple, chances were she'd found some and relayed it to Jack. That's why he'd fallen behind in the chase, despite obviously being in better shape than any of them.

"Jessica," Jack said, "I know you're pregnant."

Hands still shaking, TJ's eyes danced uncertainly toward Jessica. It appeared as though he hadn't known.

"Lower the weapon, Jessica," Austin ordered. "Now."

She didn't.

Austin searched his mind desperately for something to say. Anything to get Madge out of there and resolve this situation without anyone firing. If he fired at TJ or Jessica, he would be shooting to kill, and that could mean the automatic destruction of every medical record in Kitsap county.

"Jessica, TJ, let's make a deal," Kendall said, inching forward. "TJ, you set down your weapon and let Madge go. Jessica, you can keep your weapon. If you back up slowly onto the plane without firing it, we will let you go. You and the baby."

Austin locked eyes with TJ. "Yes, that's the only way anyone gets out of this safely. We can still end this without any bloodshed. And your baby will be safe, TJ." As Austin spoke, he was doing his best to sound calm and reasonable, but still the memory of the scene in that basement burned inside him.

He didn't just want to shoot TJ; he wanted to do something much, much worse.

Very slowly, TJ's eyes turned to Jessica. "Is this true, Jess? You have, you have our baby inside you?"

Gun still aimed at Austin, Jessica rubbed her free hand over her shirt, a nurturing gesture that highlighted an ever-so-slightly protruding abdomen for TJ. She nodded, a strange smile crossing her face. "I wanted our little girl to be a surprise for you. I was going to tell you once all of this was behind us."

"I didn't know you were..." TJ froze, blinking back tears.

"A daughter TJ," Madge said. "I regret not having children. For a while I had my Ernest, but now I have no one. Someday you'll grow old and look back on your life and wish you had someone to pass your secrets and treasures to. Money can't buy love and happiness, but having children in your life can. TJ, you may think I don't know you. But, in many ways I do. And I know that you would make a great father. Do what the officer is asking. Do this for your child. Keep your baby safe. That's your only job as its father."

Austin watched as, ever so slowly, TJ lowered the weapon.

"Crouch down and put your weapon on the ground," Austin demanded.

When he had, Austin met Madge's eyes and waved her to the side. She shuffled away before sitting heavily on the airstrip.

Gun still on Austin, Jessica backed toward the stairs of the Cessna. But then, in a movement that chilled Austin, she twisted her wrist around and pointed the gun at her own belly. "I don't trust any of you to keep your deal." Her eyes were wide and cold, darting from Austin to Jack. "I know you could shoot out the tires, send a plane after us. But we're getting out of here. Alive. And if not, the death of this child will be on your heads. I won't get taken in alive. Come after us and I'll shoot myself through the stomach. I'll kill myself *and* the baby."

She took the steps backwards, still facing them, hands shaking as she pressed the gun into her own belly. Austin kept his gun on her, but he couldn't bring himself to fire. He wasn't certain, but he thought it more likely than not that she was telling the truth, and he couldn't bring himself to let her kill the baby.

Austin saw TJ move for the gun he'd placed on the ground. Leaping forward, he kicked it out of his reach. Jack pulled out a pair of handcuffs and secured TJ, pushing his face into the ground as he lay him on his stomach.

When Austin looked back at the plane, the stairs were retracting. The plane was inching away slowly now and Jessica appeared in the cockpit window.

Lifting his face from the ground, TJ turned his head to look up into the cockpit window.

Then they all watched as Jessica leaned in and kissed the pilot on the mouth, long and slow.

Austin was stunned. What the hell was going on?

Still on the ground, TJ let out an animalistic howl. "Noooooo!"

"You got used, TJ," Jack said. "That's Jessica's husband. She *is* pregnant, but you're not the father."

The sheer quantity of pain that passed over TJ's face in the few seconds that followed was like nothing Austin had ever seen. It was as though all the agony of his life had congealed into this moment, shredding his heart, ending his soul.

For half a second, Austin thought TJ had gotten a taste of the retribution he deserved for what he'd done.

Then TJ said something Austin hadn't expected. "Her gun isn't loaded."

Austin looked from Jack to Kendall to TJ.

"I loved that woman but I never trusted her," TJ said, his voice steady, uncontrolled tears still cascading over his cheeks. "I'm gonna need some kind of deal when this is all over. You'll give it to me right? I gave her the gun. She doesn't know how to use it. It's not loaded, okay?"

"Your call," Jack said, locking eyes with Austin.

Kendall sidled up beside him. "We're taking out the wheels," she said decisively, already pulling out her weapon.

As the plane began increasing its speed, Austin, Kendall, and Jack all opened fire simultaneously, blowing the tires into rubber fragments that bounced away from the plane.

The Cessna wobbled and screeched, metallic flashes spewing from the damaged landing gear as it scraped against the runway.

The plane skidded to a stop about twenty yards away.

An odd silence followed, though Austin's ears were still ringing. "Let's board," he said. "But be careful, the pilot could also be armed."

CHAPTER FORTY-FOUR

AUSTIN RAN for the plane at breakneck speed, hoping to catch the occupants off guard. He couldn't see Jessica through the cockpit window, but the pilot appeared to have been knocked out cold. His chin rested on his chest and blood smeared the window where he'd hit his head.

Austin threw open the door on the fuselage and deployed the retractable stairs. He saw Jessica laying on the floor right by the doorway, reorienting herself after the unexpected stop, gun just out of reach. Despite what TJ had said, he had to assume it was hot.

Before he could make a move, Jessica gained control of the firearm and leveled the barrel for a killshot at Austin's chest. Austin didn't have a death wish and was left no other option than to throw up his hands.

He slowly lowered his own gun and placed it gently on the tarmac.

"You, too," Jessica screamed at Kendall and Jack, "Or I'll shoot him."

"Dennis?" Jessica called to the pilot, who didn't answer. "Dennis, are you okay?"

Gun still on Austin, she stood, reaching back into the cockpit with her free hand to shake him. "Dennis?" The man gave no response. "Dammit Dennis, you won't find me raising this baby without you." She pulled her free hand back again, this time clenching her fist to go in for a punch.

Austin stared in disbelief as she swung at him, the gun swinging wildly in the air as she struck him in the jaw with her fist. "I will not raise this baby if you're dead you lazy bastard!"

In half a second, Austin leapt up the stairs and onto the small plane, ducking down to avoid hitting his head and tackling Jessica from behind just before she could strike the pilot's face with the butt of the gun.

"My head," Dennis called out, a slur in his voice. "Jessica, bring me some aspirin, it's downstairs in the bathroom cabinet I think."

"Get your own damn aspirin," Jessica hissed back at him. "And we're not at home, you idiot."

Jack had used a pair of zip ties to secure both the pilot and Jessica. "According to my associate, Violet, the FBI has been able to solve the encryption." For the first time, Austin heard a hint of levity in Jack's voice. "Our cyber team managed to bypass the ransomware by exploiting a vulnerability in the algorithm." He appeared to be reading from his phone. "I barely know what this means, but they isolated the malware in a virtual environment, reverse-engineered its code, something something something, and generated a decryption key."

"What does any of that mean?" Austin asked.

"Especially the something something something part?" Kendall asked.

Jack shrugged. "I think it means they found themselves a virtual lockpick and broke in. All medical records are now being restored, and the attack has been neutralized."

Jack's phone rang and he stepped away to answer it.

Austin yanked Jessica up and stood her next to TJ and Dennis. As they reached the ground, Austin squinted into the bright morning sun, the fatigue hitting him as the adrenaline he'd been running on faded.

Jack reappeared behind them. "There's more, Austin. Our team was able to reverse engineer a *physical* address from the Bitcoin address the ransomware attackers used. They tracked the transaction through multiple blockchain entries, uncovering a link to a small house in Renton. The FBI just stormed the place and have caught two accomplices involved in the cyber-attack."

Jessica groaned. "Stupid bastards. Why did I trust such a bunch of imbeciles."

Kendall was standing beside Madge, who'd been sitting on a pile of lifejackets from the FBI boat.

Madge hadn't said anything in a long time, but she appeared to be okay, if exhausted. She stood slowly. Then, without warning, she lunged forward, swinging something at Jessica. For half an instant, Austin thought it was a gun, but the leathery *smack* sound it made as it struck Jessica's face told Austin it was actually a shoe.

Jessica rocked back, her face reddening.

Madge said, "You messed with the wrong lady."

Kendall, clearly suppressing a smile, took Madge by the arm and led her away, mumbling something half-heartedly about how they can't let her assault a restrained suspect.

A few hundred yards away, in an open field, a helicopter was landing. There was a lot of mess to clean up, but it appeared, for now, this case was over.

CHAPTER FORTY-FIVE

Three weeks later

THE BRIGHT MORNING sun was beaming through the window of what would be his father's new room in the memory care section of Seaside Cedars Retirement Community.

"This restaurant has good toast," Austin's father said. He was still getting used to the new environment and because he wasn't upset, Austin ignored his statement.

"I'm glad you like it here, Dad," Austin said, smiling.

It had taken a couple weeks, but a spot had freed up at Seaside Cedars, and now his dad would be within a forty-five-minute drive. Though the facility in Seattle had been perfectly fine, this one would make it easier for Austin to see his parents, and he was happy about that.

While Olivia performed almost all the managerial roles on site, a temporary director—borrowed from a sister facility—would work remotely while the board searched for a replacement for Jessica, who was now awaiting trial along with TJ, Dennis, and Christine. Because she had provided evidence on TJ as well as information that had helped lead to their capture, Christine would likely receive a deal.

"Honey, let's have breakfast here every day," Austin's mom said. "I'll be here every morning."

"And sometimes I'll join you," Austin added. "As often as I can."

His mother had taken a one-bedroom apartment in a waterfront condo nearby. It was only a five-minute walk to the facility and, Austin had to admit to himself, the arrangement made sense. His father often had only ten or twenty lucid minutes a day. His care needs had increased significantly, and this facility was full of wonderful caregivers. When Austin and his mother toured the place before moving him in, they had been impressed—his father liking the toast had been the icing on the cake.

All six of the men and women who had been pulled from the basement dungeon had survived. Some had already been released and admitted to Seaside Cedars Retirement Community. The two who were still in the hospital being treated for wounds and malnutrition would join them as soon as they were well enough to do so.

Madge Evering had committed over two million dollars to pay for all of them to live at the facility. And not only that, Christine's mother Crystal would be moving into Seaside Cedars Retirement Community as well.

After hours of questioning and over a week of digging through old files and communications, Crystal had been cleared of any wrongdoing. It turned out she had been ignorant of what was going on. Usually locked in the attic, she'd been a victim like the others. In fact, she'd been suffering from a severe B12 deficiency, which manifested as dementia. But once that was taken care of and she realized what had gone on in her business, under her roof, she was devastated. Furthermore, she was able to offer mountains of evidence against both Christine and TJ. And she was feeling much better.

It turned out that Helen Virginia Fullman—the earliest victim who'd been found under the Deception Pass Bridge —had been murdered by TJ and his neighbor Forest in the trailer park. It had started as a less nefarious scheme; they hadn't set out to kill her at first. The men had hatched a simple plan to steal most of her Social Security money. When she figured it out and confronted them, the argument had turned into a struggle. The struggle ended when TJ held a pillow over her head until she died. Hoping to cover their tracks, they had dumped the body over Deception Pass Bridge. That also explained why she hadn't had any of the bruises or binding marks that the prisoners in the dungeon had.

TJ and Forest had continued to cash her checks until they'd been flagged and, when her death had been ruled an accident, the case had gone away and they'd been forced into a repayment plan.

TJ's neighbor Forest had been wracked with guilt ever since, unwilling to turn himself in, but also not descending into further darkness.

TJ, on the other hand, had used the murder of Fullman as an inspiration for further evil. Using his experience with the Social Security checks as a starting point, TJ had convinced Christine to use her mother's facility to take advantage of the elderly in every way imaginable. This included promising Hank Butterfield a lifetime room at their facility for a one-time payment of $25,000, which had been every penny Butterfield had to his name. The same day TJ had cashed the check—before Butterfield had even packed a bag—TJ had suffocated him and tossed his body off the Manette Bridge.

While working at Seaside Cedars, TJ had connected

with Jessica, and the two of them had hatched the plan to kidnap Madge and take her to Mexico, where they would live the high life on her millions of dollars. They'd planned to dispose of her there. But Jessica and her husband Dennis had planned to go even bigger, to double-cross TJ and add another five million dollars in bitcoin to the scheme by hacking the region's medical records.

On his way out of the facility, Austin spotted Madge and Crystal sitting next to a large indoor plant conversing quietly.

"Hi ladies, how are you feeling?" Austin asked with a smile.

"Better, much better," Madge said.

"My heart is broken, but I'm feeling better and better every minute," Crystal said, bringing a tissue to the corner of her eye to catch a tear.

Madge reached over and patted her on the hand. "Just because they can break our hearts by sabotaging their own lives, doesn't mean we are responsible for what our children do in this world my dear. But now the destruction is over. And..." Madge directed her attention to Austin, "we have you, Kendall, and Jack to thank for making it possible for healing to begin. Where is Kendall, anyway? Isn't she your partner?"

"She is," Austin said. "She's at the beach with Ralph."

"Oh, I bet Ralph must be *very* handsome. But I assumed she was single," Madge said. "I don't know why."

"Actually, she *is* single," Austin explained. "Ralph is a handsome animal, but he's her corgi. In our line of work, you're always hit with a little guilt when you spend too much time away from your furry friends. She's taking a couple days off to throw sticks."

"Good for her," Madge said.

"I'll be doing the same," Austin said.

"You deserve it, Mr. Austin," Crystal said. "And again, I can't thank you enough for saving my residents. I wish I had been able to stop this all from happening in the first place. I'll never forgive myself."

"I'm glad I was able to help you and those people this time," Austin said. "And Crystal, none of us are perfect. All you can do now is make amends to those people as they move in. Work to earn *their* forgiveness." After a heavy silence, he continued. "My father just moved in as well. You two are neighbors." Austin smiled. "He'll be in the memory care wing. If you see him, say hi and make sure he gets as much toast as he likes. He loves the bread here."

"They bake it fresh every day," Madge said.

"Consider it done," Crystal said, nodding and smiling.

Austin reached out and put a hand on Madge's shoulder. "I heard what you did, offering to pay for everyone to move in here."

Madge smiled sadly. "I have been more fortunate than I probably deserve in this life. I didn't see what was inside that room when I was strapped to that chair. But I smelled it, and I heard about the details." She paused, shaking her head. "I decided I wanted to give away my money with a warm hand. If I'm going to be a target because of what I have, I thought I should give to the good people in my life in case the bad people are more successful the next time around. I'm going to cancel my champagne cruises for a while and let everyone who couldn't otherwise afford it move in on my dime. Anyway, I have enough money to live here until I'm two hundred and fifty, and I don't think I'll be around for that many more years."

"I don't know, Madge, having seen what you went through and seeing you now..." Austin said, looking her up and down holding his chin in a mock assessment gesture. "I wouldn't be shocked if you're still center stage at your two hundred fiftieth birthday party."

"Let's hope not," Madge said. Her laughter expressed utter delight and the youthful twinkle in her eye conveyed she was about to say something clever. "I don't think they make cakes sturdy enough for that many candles."

Out front, as he got into his car, Austin saw Lucy and Jimmy leading Lucy's mother across the parking lot.

He nodded at Jimmy, but didn't stop to say hello, knowing they'd see each other again soon.

After all the hoopla, it had turned out that Lucy's mother didn't want to live with them in the first place.

Jimmy had laughed when he told Austin the story—she'd met with Lucy in confidence and wanted her to let him down gently—she'd rather live around people her own age. She wanted to play bingo, go to the famous trivia brunches, and even meet some friends to travel with, but had been worried about hurting Jimmy's feelings. Thankfully their marriage was saved. This time.

Seaside Cedars Retirement Community would be getting another new resident. Lucy's mother had already picked out her room.

CHAPTER FORTY-SIX

The Next Day

THE PRESS CONFERENCE was going to take place in the large meeting room at the Kitsap Sheriff's Department. Austin sat on a little riser behind a folding table that had been covered with a black cloth. Kendall sat next to him.

Jimmy and Lucy leaned against the wall, watching, smiles across their faces, as Ridley made his way through the small gaggle of reporters and stood in front of the podium.

"Ladies and gentlemen, today we honor two exceptional individuals whose bravery and dedication have made a tremendous impact on our community. Kendall Shaw and Thomas Austin, through their relentless pursuit of justice, have successfully dismantled a heinous criminal gang that preyed upon the elderly and threatened the medical records of Kitsap County. Their actions have saved countless lives and ensured the safety and well-being of our most vulnerable citizens. It is my great honor to present them with this official state commendation, recognizing their heroism and

unwavering commitment to the people of Kitsap County.
We are forever grateful for their service and sacrifice."

Austin had insisted that Jack Russo from the FBI be
honored as well, but Jack had demurred. It wasn't appro-
priate for an FBI agent to receive this sort of local fanfare,
and eventually, he'd accepted Austin's sincere thanks
instead.

Ridley waited for the polite applause to die down. "Now,
I would like to call to the podium," he said, "Deputy
County Commissioner Marty Larsen, who will add some
words."

Larsen lowered the microphone about ten inches,
thanked Ridley profusely, and then looked out at the
reporters like a king surveying his subjects. "I've always said,
excellent law enforcement is the backbone of the success of
this great community..."

Austin tuned him out. He already knew what was
coming next. Larsen would officially welcome Austin as a
valued member of the Kitsap County Sheriff's Department
and would vow that increased funding for the department
would be placed into the budget over the next five years. He
would also announce that all planned hearings on the
department's actions would be canceled, as would all
appearances of Gretchen Vale before the county
commission.

In exchange, the department wouldn't try to embarrass
him publicly for his recent jack-assery, and they'd allow him
to take some of the credit for the takedown of Jessica, TJ,
Dennis, Christine, and the others. He'd also make it his
personal mission to allow Carla Rivera to return to her dive
shop and, eventually, take the oath to become a U.S. citizen.
He had a brother with the immigration office, and had
promised he could get it done.

Ridley had brokered the deal, trying to bring peace

between the department and the county commissioners, and Austin had eventually relented. Of course, his first instinct had been to object, to try to kick Larsen while he was down, but in the end, he didn't care.

Larsen's political maneuvering was just part of the land-scape, and if it meant better funding for the department and a smoother transition for himself, Austin was willing to let it slide.

Austin wasn't part of the scattering of the ashes, but he watched it all from a dozen yards away, sitting on a drift-wood log. Timothy Vernon Steele was only 22 years old, the great-nephew of Flagg Michael Steele, the 99-year-old Navy Seabee whose body Carla Rivera had discovered under the Deception Pass bridge.

It had taken Sheriff Derby two weeks to track down the only known relative of the deceased, but he'd finally found Timothy, and it turned out he lived only a few hours away. Austin had been eager to put the name to the John Doe and had offered to deliver the death notification if his identity and family could be identified. The young man had asked that his great uncle be cremated and, although most of his ashes would be officially buried at Arlington National Cemetery, he asked Austin if he could scatter some of them on the beach in front of his store.

Austin, of course, had happily obliged.

After the young man scattered the ashes, Austin fed him a burger and fries with a beer on the house.

Later that evening, Austin lay awake in bed, wondering whether he'd done enough to honor Flagg Michael Steele's service in World War Two. He decided he had. Helping to avenge his death, combined with the simple act of feeding his great-nephew, was a gesture a Seabee would have appreciated.

Maybe, like Austin himself, Steele wouldn't have wanted much fanfare.

～

It was going to be a fabulous summer. Austin's café, general store, and bait shop were busier than ever.

Since he was now receiving a salary from the county of Kitsap, he had made his former sous chef, Andy, a partner in the business. Andy was now the head chef of the restaurant, the day-to-day manager of the store, and took a percentage of all the profits earned by the business as a whole. He'd even spent much of the last six months finishing a business degree online. Austin had given him one directive: don't make the place too fancy. The food was good, the beer was cold, and this summer it would be full of both locals and snowbirds returning for the season, as well as tourists who came to walk the beaches at Point No Point or Foulweather Bluff.

Austin hadn't lived here long, but he felt a responsibility to the community to make the store whatever they wanted it to be. Now, as he sat at a little metal table out front, watching the people come and go, he was happier than he'd been in years. Ralph and Run lay next to each other beside a metallic water bowl. They'd had a good hour on the beach together and now they were ready for a long nap.

Kendall returned from the store to join Austin at the table. Setting a cold beer down in front of him, she took a swig from her own as she sat.

"This really is the life here," she said.

A large black SUV with tinted windows pulled up. It was not the kind of vehicle Austin saw much out this way. The engine turned off and a young man in a navy blue suit got out and opened the door. The massive frame of Ridley Calvin emerged.

It had been some time since Austin had seen him dressed down. He was wearing well-fitted jeans and a white button-down. He breathed the air in deeply, as though appreciating the fresh scent of the beach. Crossing the parking lot in a few easy strides, he pulled up a chair and sat next to Kendall.

"Beer?" Austin asked.

"Don't mind if I do," Ridley said, accepting the bottle Austin hadn't yet touched. He took a long pull. "What is it about you, Austin, that you always get the wildest cases?"

Austin shook his head. "I really don't know."

"Kind of makes me miss Kitsap," Ridley said. "You know, I never really wanted to become governor. The only way I was finally convinced to do it was when I learned the details of the other two jackasses running. God knows no government is perfect. The longer I spend in the capital, the more I learn that the best I can do is try to make things a fraction of a percent better than they would be if I wasn't there. I've got a lot less power than I thought I'd have."

"I bet you're doing an excellent job," Kendall said.

"Damn right he is," Austin agreed. "The older I get, the more I think the best we can hope for is to have decent people in the important jobs and just let them do their best."

He took a sip of his beer, which tasted of crisp hops and malty sweetness. It was damn near perfect. A car door closed nearby and Run woke up halfway to her feet. Then, seeing Austin shrug, she lay down and fell back asleep immediately.

Kendall stood. "I'm going to get us some more beers."

Ridley stood as well. "And I'm going to head in and use the restroom. It was a long drive."

When they were gone, Austin stared out at the water for a long moment, his view finally interrupted by a taxi pulling into the spot next to Ridley's SUV. He wasn't sure, but he thought he recognized the long black hair through the back windshield.

A moment later, Sy emerged, standing for a long time before looking at him. It was as though she was settling in, adjusting to what was about to be her new life.

They'd spoken every day since the case ended. She'd gotten an internship at a winery in central Washington, where she was going to work two days a week for the next six months. She'd also gotten a short-term lease on a two-bedroom apartment in a new development in Kingston, only five minutes from Claire Anderson's house. Austin had offered for her to stay with him, but she insisted on getting her own place, and Austin had eventually agreed that it was probably for the best. This was serious now, but they were going to take things slow.

Sy turned around slowly and walked across the parking lot. She wore a light blue dress and white polka dot scarf that was perfect for summer. Austin stood. Run looked up again, then, seeing Sy, leapt up.

When Sy reached the table, she crouched down, greeting Run before even acknowledging Austin's presence. He didn't mind. Run demanded immediate attention, after all. When Run had finished her inspection of Sy, she lay back down next to Ralph and Austin opened his arms wide.

Sy hugged him for a long time. "Oh, I almost forgot," she said, pulling away and jogging across the parking lot.

Returning, Austin saw that she held a clear bag full of red and yellow Rainier cherries.

"Those are my favorite," Austin said.

"First of the season, at least from what the guy at the ferry dock farmer's market told me. You know you guys have stands here where you can buy a bag of these for three bucks?"

Austin laughed. "I know. Pretty sure that's the main reason I moved here."

He popped a cherry in his mouth. It was sweet and tart and as good as he'd hoped. He tossed the pit in the garbage can outside the front door of his store.

"It's going to be a good summer," he said.

"It absolutely is," Sy agreed.

—The End—

If you enjoyed this book, continue the series with Thomas Austin #10: The Vanishing at Opal Creek (releasing September, 2024)

A NOTE FROM THE AUTHOR

Thanks for reading!

Thomas Austin and I have three things in common. First, we both live in a small beach town not far from Seattle. Second, we both like to cook. And third, we both spend more time than we should talking to our corgis.

If you enjoyed this book, I encourage you to check out the whole series of Thomas Austin novels online. Each book can be read as a standalone, although relationships and situations develop from book to book, so they will be more enjoyable if read in order.

And if you're loving the Thomas Austin series, check out my new series of fast-paced Pacific Northwest mysteries: FBI Task Force S.W.O.R.D.

I also have an online store, where you can buy signed paperbacks, mugs, t-shirts, and more featuring Thomas Austin's lovable corgi, Run, as well as locations and quotations from all my books. Check that out on my website.

Every day I feel fortunate to be able to wake up and create characters and write stories. And that's all made possible by readers like you. So, again, I extend my heartfelt thanks for checking out my books, and I wish you hundreds of hours of happy reading to come.

D.D. Black

MORE D.D. BLACK NOVELS

The Thomas Austin Crime Thrillers

Book 1: *The Bones at Point No Point*

Book 2: *The Shadows of Pike Place*

Book 3: *The Fallen of Foulweather Bluff*

Book 4: *The Horror at Murden Cove*

Book 5: *The Terror in The Emerald City*

Book 6: *The Drowning at Dyes Inlet*

Book 7: *The Nightmare at Manhattan Beach*

Book 8: *The Silence at Mystery Bay*

Book 9: *The Darkness at Deception Pass*

Book 10: *The Vanishing at Opal Creek*

FBI Task Force S.W.O.R.D.

Book 1: *The Fifth Victim*

Book 2: *We Forget Nothing*

Book 3: *Widows of Medina*

Standalone Crime Novels

The Things She Stole

ABOUT D.D. BLACK

D.D. Black is the author of the Thomas Austin Crime Thrillers, the FBI Task Force S.W.O.R.D. series, and other Pacific Northwest crime novels. When he's not writing, he can be found strolling the beaches of the Pacific Northwest, cooking dinner for his wife and kids, or throwing a ball for his corgi over and over and over. Find out more at ddblack author.com.

ABOUT THE AUTHOR

Made in the USA
Monee, IL
14 October 2024